WEDDING DAY AND FOUL PLAY

A CONSIGNMENT SHOP MYSTERY

DUFFY BROWN

PRAISE FOR DUFFY

Characters are incredibly colorful! A delightfully Cozy!
The Cozy Pages

If you enjoy cozy mysteries and you love interesting settings, then Duffy Brown will be right up your alley. I can't wait for the next Cycle Path Mystery to come out.
The Book Connection

I didn't want the book to end! After the exciting showdown as well as the sweetest ending though, I can't wait for more!
Cuddle Up With a Cozy Mystery

A humorous and engaging cozy mystery. Duffy Brown has a writing style that I classify as easy breezy. It is light, has humor, good dialogue and steady pacing.
The Avid Reader

I'm usually pretty good as figuring out "whodunit" in mystery books, but this one had me guessing until near the very end. Congratulations, Ms. Brown, you had me fooled.

DEAR READER

Hi Everyone and Welcome to Savannah

Reagan and Walker are getting married and there is nothing more beautiful than an Southern wedding. I love Savannah. My daughter went to school at Savannah College of Art and Design, and I fell in love with the city. When I started writing The Consignment Shop Mysteries, I knew I had to set the series here.

There are twenty-three squares with enormous live oaks right in the heart of the city, and once you park your car you can walk from one end of Savannah to the other. The restaurants are amazing, and I refer to a lot of them in the stories. Yes, there is really a Zunzi's with their amazing conquistador sandwiches, The Telfair Museum is amazing, The Old Pirate House is truly haunted, and I have put away more than my share of martinis at Jen's and Friends.

Time moves slower in Savannah. My daughter used to call it Slow-vannah. In spring the azaleas are as big as a bus and the magnolias the size of a dinner plate. And, of course, the whole city smells like heaven. In August the humidity is so high it curls your hair, and in the fall the city is ablaze with Crape Myrtle.

So, here's to Reagan and Walker and BW... May they live long, laugh much and fall in love more each day.

Hugs, Duffy

CHAPTER 1

"One hundred and eighty-three days and fourteen hours without tripping across a dead body and tomorrow I--Reagan Summerside, former bum-magnet--am getting married right here in Savannah to the best guy ever," I gushed to Auntie KiKi. The two of us gazed around her pristine Victorian adorned with a bazillion of my fave yellow and white mums, twinkling lights, and satin-clad chairs in neat rows. "I'm not sure which is more amazing."

Auntie KiKi's smile wobbled then she burst into tears.

"Wait! No." I rushed over and put my arm around her. "You're not losing a niece. You're gaining a nephew-in-law. My getting married is a good thing, at least this time it is. I'm *not* marrying bed-hopping Hollis like before, and I *am* marrying Walker Boone. Boone, Bruce Willis, and I are living right next door to you in Cherry House and intend to mooch dinner and doggy treats every chance we get. In two weeks, it's Uncle Putter's birthday, and we'll have a party with cake and ice cream and be one big happy family."

"Oh, honey," Auntie KiKi sputtered, "I'm afraid we won't be getting the chance to do any of that. Lord have mercy and saints preserve us nothing is ever going to be the same around here again."

"It's going to be better." I hugged her a little tighter. "All the wedding hoopla will be behind us even though I didn't want hoopla in the first place."

Auntie KiKi sniffed and arched her left brow. "This from the bride who picked a dress with enough blush tulle to cover three states."

Auntie KiKi was my one and only auntie and second mamma since the day Daddy went wild boar hunting with the good old boys including Jim Beam. Auntie KiKi was also my partner in crime. It was a predicament we didn't choose but that sort of fell into our laps starting with the day we found a dead body in a car trunk. Together, we now figured out whodunit while sitting on my front porch with martinis in hand, accompanied by one, two, or even three olives, depending on how dire the situation or how stumped we happened to be at the time.

"Everything is perfect for tomorrow. Okay, the bridesmaid dresses are fuchsia. I got roped into that, along with having a police detective in the wedding and Coroner Carver as an usher, though he did promise not to hand out *You're Dying to Meet Me* business cards."

"And think about this," I galloped on. "We all just had a lovely rehearsal dinner at the Pirate House, you're walking me down the aisle tomorrow at five p.m. sharp and BW is the ring bearer. Mamma is officiating under that gorgeous white rose arch in front of the fireplace, and we convinced her to wear the sage dress instead of the red one she insisted on."

"I still don't understand why my Princess isn't part of the wedding party." Auntie KiKi sniffed.

Maybe because darling Princess morphed into the snarling, hissing, biting cat from hell when Auntie KiKi wasn't looking, though she would never believe such a thing. "Just look around here." I waved my hand through the air in triumph. "We couldn't squeeze one more bow or mum into this house if we tried."

"Wanna bet?" came a voice behind us. I spun around to face Cornelius McBride of the I Do Declare auction house, standing in the doorway. Corny wasn't a friend but more of a business acquaintance for when a notable antique needed to be bought or sold. "No matter what the occasion, Miss KiKi, there's always a little business that needs tending to at the last minute."

"Don't you 'Miss KiKi' me, you scalawag, no-good, horse-stealing, jackass! You have no right to be here." Auntie KiKi snagged a wrought-iron candle stand off the floor and jabbed it at Corny as the candle rolled under a chair. "Skedaddle, or I'll skewer you like a big, fat rat shish kebab and display your remains on my front lawn like a trophy."

I grabbed the stand and set it back on the floor. "You have to excuse my auntie." I flashed Corny a weak smile. "Weddings are stressful times, and we're all tired and a little cranky. So if this is about that pie safe you sold for Auntie last week and her not being happy with the price, maybe we can deal with it at another time."

I sat KiKi in one of the chairs. "I know Mr. McBride didn't get as much as you wanted for the safe but not everyone needs to be saving pies these days with the Cakery Bakery right around the corner. Maybe you're overreacting just a tad, and if Mr. McBride will come back next week we can deal with-"

"The only dealing that varmint does is from the bottom of the deck and I'd like nothing more than to separate his head from his shoulders in one fell swoop."

"Seems a mite extreme for a pie safe," I muttered while hunkering down to look for the candle. Not in any hurry to leave, Corny leaned lazily against the entrance to the ballroom where Auntie KiKi expertly taught foxtrot, waltz and the occa-sional tango to those bound for cotillions and anniversary celebrations. Tonight, the room was set with round tables, white china and linens. Tomorrow the most delicious wedding cake ever would grace the table in the corner.

I set the candle on the stand and adjusted the white satin bow. Corny raked back his black toupee that didn't quite match his gray-streaked hair. It left a telltale ring around his head which sort of looked like a halo, or maybe devil horns, depending on your point of view.

"Is there something else we can help you with?" I asked, trying to get Corny out of the house.

"Always liked this house." Corny wrinkled his nose and curled his lip. "It's got fine bones as they say. But I'm not the one needing help. I'm the one offering help. I'm here to make your dear old auntie's worst nightmare go away."

Nightmare! That was not the word a soon-to-be-bride wanted to hear. "I have a terrific wedding dress, a terrific guy, and a terrific venue and no nightmares," I said, mostly to reassure myself that everything was okay because suddenly things felt like they weren't okay at all.

"Venue? Funny you should mention that." Corny snapped a yellow mum from the big white urn of overflowing blooms. He twirled the stem between his fingers.

Auntie KiKi growled, "You gave me your word. We agreed that you'd keep all this quiet till after the wedding."

"You mean like on the day after tomorrow, when this here house no longer belongs to the likes of you and the doc but to somebody else. From the look on Reagan's face, my guess is she has no idea what I'm talking about."

"You remember that old sea chest?" Corny said to me. "The one you found in your attic when renovating Cherry House. The one you gave me to sell. When I cleaned it out, I came across a deed stuck in the burlap lining. It wasn't just any old deed, but one proclaiming that Thaddeus Beauregard Vanderpool gambled away this here beloved home known as Rosegate in a poker game to one Jeremiah Beaumont. It happened right down there at the Pirate House on Broad Street where you were tonight." Corny added an unsettling laugh that made the hair on my arms stand on end.

"June 12, 1867, I do believe," he went on. "Signed and witnessed, filed at the courthouse just like it should be. Then Jeremiah got himself shot dead in a duel, the courthouse burned clean to the ground, and papers went missing...till now."

"Waitaminute." I held up my hands as if stopping a freight train running full steam ahead. "What are you talking about? What deed? Rosegate belongs to Auntie KiKi and Uncle Putter."

Auntie KiKi smoothed her hand over her lavender dress and readjusted the little matching hat. "It's true, honey, every blasted word. Walker and your Uncle Putter tried for months to find a loophole in the deed transfer and got nowhere. That's what they were doing all those late nights when I suspected Putter was stepping out on me. Fact is, he and Walker were meeting up in Walker's law office trying to fix things and spare me any upsetment on losing this here house that I love."

"But...but this happened over a hundred years ago. There's got to be a statute of limitations on the temporary insanity of drunk men betting the family home?"

"A deed is a deed, girly girl." Corny slipped the mum into the lapel buttonhole of his wrinkled tweed jacket. "And the deed in the chest is the verified original." Corny flashed a tobacco-stained smile. "But there's no need to fret. All is not lost. I do have some good news. Right now, there are only five people in the whole wide world who know about this deed and for a somewhat reasonable price I'm willing to forget about its very existence. I'll go back to my place over at the auction house and you stay here in your nice house and life goes on like it always has...more or less."

"More for you and less for Auntie KiKi, every time you feel the need. My guess is that Uncle Putter and Boone told you to take a flying leap, and you're thinking Auntie KiKi will cave and pay you off?"

"Unless she intends to lose the home that's been in the Vanderpool family for five generations to a less desirable someone else."

"Six generations," Auntie KiKi said with a sigh.

I added, "So who's this someone else? Maybe they'll sell Rosegate back to Auntie Kiki and Uncle Putter? These big old money-pit Victorians aren't everyone's cup of tea. There's always a leak in the roof somewhere, a burst pipe, termites, squirrels in the attic and to tell you the truth I can't really think of any Savannah families who date back a hundred and thirty years that I dislike as much as you're letting on except...except..." The room started to spin, my eyes not focusing. I couldn't breathe. "Did you say Jeremiah Beaumont?

"Making Hollis Beaumont, your horse's patoot of an ex who did the horizontal hula on your very own dining room table with Cupcake the first, or was that Cupcake the second? Hard to keep his cupcakes straight without a scorecard...the one who inherits Rosegate."

Corny snorted. "It's adieu Auntie dearest and hello hula Hollis." He polished the diamond signet ring on his pinkie finger against his jacket sleeve. No doubt the ring was conned from some other poor unsuspecting customer he had the goods on.

"First thing tomorrow morning," Corny said, "I'm telling Hula Boy to call the movers to come move in unless you pay up tonight."

Auntie KiKi pursed her lips, her eyes beady. "If Gillespie or your sister knew what you were up to, they'd skin you alive."

"My stupid partner has nothing to say about the auction

house these days. My dumpy sister is so taken with her fiancée she doesn't give two flying farts about anything but getting married."

Auntie KiKi jumped to her feet. "I should do the world a big old favor and shoot you dead on the spot. I'll bet dollars to doughnuts I'm not the first person you've tried to bamboozle."

"Those are some big words for a Southern lady like yourself who's in a mighty tough spot," Corny scoffed while Auntie KiKi stomped toward the hallway.

"Mr. McGuire, you should never underestimate a Southern lady," Walker Boone said as he strolled into the room looking more delish than any man had a right to in soft jeans and a white dress shirt. His forever five o'clock scruff had morphed into eleven o'clock stubble; the thin scar across his right eye and his not-so-straight nose, left over from his Seventeenth Street gang days, only added to his to-die-for handsomeness...in my humble, very biased, and deeply in love opinion.

"I think you need to leave now, McGuire," Boone said in a low steely voice.

Corny swallowed hard his coloring more wallpaper paste than sunshine Savannah. "You being some fancy lawyer now don't scare me none, Walker Boone. I'll be back and I'll have Hollis Beaumont with me. The law's the law even for the rich. Enjoy your wedding 'cause it's the last thing the Vanderpools will be doing here except packing up and shipping out."

Boone took a step forward, Corny scrambled out the front door and Auntie KiKi went for the fireplace. She grabbed the Vanderpool double-barrel shotgun from the Civil War, headed for the door and aimed it square at Corny's bony retreating butt. "You won't be back here ever," she yelled, "or anyplace else, if I have anything to say about it."

"No!" I yelled as Boone grabbed the shotgun barrel diverting it toward the ceiling and *kaboom* blasting though the hall. Plaster chunks rained down around the three of us and Corny was halfway down the block before the dust cleared.

"You, Walker Boone," Auntie KiKi sputtered while straightening her hat, "are a first-rate party pooper. I could have finished that varmint off and planted his sorry self in the garden. It's been done, you know."

"I do know," Boone said. He waved his hand through the air to chase away the dust. "I was there. And where are you headed for now?" he called after Auntie KiKi hoofing her way toward the front door.

"Putter had emergency heart surgery and I simply refuse to sit here all alone in my house that's soon not to be my house. I'm heading for a three-olive martini to try and figure out what to do next, and you lovebirds need to be getting some sleep. Tomorrow's the big day, and no one nohow is getting in the way of that. I can promise you."

Auntie KiKi slammed the door behind her, more plaster falling from the ceiling. I turned to Boone. "We should have eloped."

"Gives a whole new meaning to 'shotgun wedding.'" Boone brushed white grit off my blue dress then put the shotgun back over the fireplace.

"Since half the neighborhood isn't on our doorstep right now wondering what's going on, my guess is this isn't KiKi's first encounter with a shootout at Rosegate Corral."

"Terrance Mayhue tried to stiff her for six months of dance lessons last year, and there's that nurse who kept making googoo eyes at Uncle Putter. No one's seen her for a while, and no one dares to ask why."

I headed for the kitchen to find a broom. "I need to call Mamma, so she doesn't hear about this deed situation secondhand. If you have any ideas what to do next, that would be great."

I opened the pantry door for the boom and dustpan as Boone came up behind me. He kissed me on the neck, sending shivers up my spine. "Sweething, I got lots of ideas on what to do next, and I guarantee they're great."

I handed him the dustpan and he arched his left brow. "Not the response I was hoping for. You're flipping your hair and your eye's twitching, so I'm thinking you have a plan?"

I placed my palms on his chest, his broad strong chest. I could feel his heart beating and wondered how I got so lucky to have this man in my life. "I have a bad plan. Hollis has always been fuming mad that I got Cherry House in our divorce settlement." We headed for the plaster pit. "So, what if I give him Cherry House in place of Rosegate?"

Boone kissed me on the forehead then knelt down and held the dustpan while I swept. "A noble gesture to be sure. Except that Cherry House is half the size of Rosegate, your Prissy Fox Consignment Shop is on the first floor, and I can't see Hollis peddling handbags and garden party dresses."

"I'll figure out something but there's more."

Boone stood and grinned, his eyes dancing. "More of what we started in the pantry?"

"Better." I put down the broom and headed for the ballroom.

"For future reference," he called after me, "there is no better."

I came back and handed him a box wrapped in white embossed paper with a gold ribbon. "I wanted to give you a special wedding gift."

"As the song says, I Got You Babe." Boone tore off the paper to a brass plaque. He read, "Walker House, Savannah, Georgia."

"It was either that or Boone's Bungalow, and this sounds classier. You are now half-owner. Well, actually you're a third owner with BW and me. We took a vote. You're the one who restored the attic to make our living space bigger. We now have two bathrooms, an adorable kitchen, you built BW his own nap nook, and you made me a real checkout counter for the Prissy Fox that is not a door propped across two chairs. Since your name is now on the deed, I can't give Walker House away without you agreeing to...to..." A tear slid down my cheek, and Boone wiped it away.

"You love Cherry House."

"Auntie KiKi came to Rosegate as a new bride and taught dance lessons in the little ballroom to put Uncle Putter through med school. You have your big, beautiful house on Montgomery Square. You can keep your law office on the first floor, and we can live on the second and third floors. We'll put the Walker House plaque on the door there, and I'll find a storefront for the Prissy Fox closer to the historic district."

Boone kissed me hard, his lips warm and reassuring that everything would somehow work out, or at least they had half a chance of working out. "This is why I love you," he murmured.

"You love me 'cause I make great SpaghettiOs surprise."

His lips smiled against mine, a touch of mischief in his dark eyes.

"Trust me, Sweething, the reason I love you is not because of SpaghettiOs surprise. But I don't have a better solution, and I did explore every legal angle. Are you sure?"

"If you take care of things here, BW and I will take care of Hollis. I found BW, abandoned, half-starved, and huddled under the porch when we were both broken. We shared McNuggets that night and saved each other. We'll get through this too."

"Good luck."

"*That* I already have, big boy." I stood on my tiptoes and kissed Boone. "I'm marrying you and like Auntie KiKi said, nothing can get in the way of that."

CHAPTER 2

"I'll have to do some fast talking but we're all going to be okay," I reassured BW while we headed for Hollis's townhouse. Night strolls with BW around Forsyth Fountain all lit up made me feel happy and content. Tonight, sprinkle doughnuts with a side of Snickers and a praline couldn't accomplish that.

We trudged on with moonlight slipping through massive branches of live oaks draped in Spanish moss. Wrought-iron streetlights cast a golden glow over sidewalks uneven from bulging tree roots older than Mamma and me put together. St. John's church chimed out eleven o'clock and all is well. If only.

"I know you love Cherry House," I added trying to keep my voice positive for BW, "but think of this. Boone's place faces Montgomery Square." I hitched my yellow pleather purse higher onto my shoulder.

"That's a pretty snooty address, and we'll be sittin' in the high cotton as Grandma Summerside used to say. We'll do some decorating beyond Boone's leather couch and big-screen TV, get white wicker furniture for the verandas and add hanging ferns and some of those little palm trees. And guess what? That cute little poodle with the pink bows lives around the corner. That's a good thing, right? You'll meet up on walks, go to the park, have playdates."

BW didn't answer. His head just dropped lower, his tail completely wagles.

"Okay, okay. This sucks, I get it. But there's nothing else to do. We have to save Uncle Putter and Auntie KiKi. If they lose their house, they'll be brokenhearted. We owe them. Who else makes you doggie peanut butter treats from scratch and... Holy cow, is that Mamma up ahead in the gazebo? What is she doing in Whitfield Square this time of night? And she's with some guy! What's Mamma doing with a guy? She a respected judge and should be home watching Judge Judy."

BW and I crouched down behind a rhododendron. I parted the branches and we stared through the dark to the adorable, little white gazebo.

"Is that Judge Swain?" I whispered to BW. "It is! They call him the Silver Fox, and he has his arms around Mamma," I seethed. "She must have met up with him after the rehearsal dinner. I should deck him." BW licked my face in agreement. "I should tell him 'Hands off, dude, I don't care how great your hair is.'" I swallowed hard. "I should leave him alone 'cause Mamma's smiling, and now she's laughing."

The judge took Mamma in a little waltz then spinning in a circle like something out of *Holiday Inn* or *Singing in the Rain* that Mamma and I watched together a bazillion times. Swain was no Fred Astaire, but he wasn't half bad either and Mamma...well, she obviously loved it. Fact is, I'd never seen her so happy, not even when I finally passed biology.

"When did all *this* happen?" I asked BW. "Right in front of our noses," I answered my own question, "with me too wrapped up in my wedding to notice."

Feeling depressed to the bone at losing my house and not

being more in tune with Mamma and what was going on in her life...some daughter I was...BW and inched our way back to the street.

"Think I should ask him to the wedding?" BW and I passed Calhoun Square, one of twenty-two beloved squares scattered throughout the city. There used to be twenty-four until the need for parking plucked away two of the squares, and citizens started chaining themselves to trees and fountains in protest of losing more.

"Then again," I added, "maybe Mamma already asked Swain as her plus-one. It's hard to wrap my brain around Mamma and a plus-one. I need to change my brain."

I took the curved iron steps to the door of a recent reno row-house that held on to its Savannah charm with Palladian windows and arched fanlights. I pulled in a deep breath, knocked, and Hollis Beaumont the third flung open the door, glass of wine in hand, party chatter in the background. He stopped short, his brown eyes widening in surprise. "What the heck are you doing here? Aren't you getting married tomorrow or something?"

Hollis closed the door behind him, hitched his hip onto the railing, and sipped his wine. A sleazy grin slid across his face. "Just couldn't stay away, huh?"

"Unfortunately, that is true." I gave BW a pat. "I have a proposition for you."

"Well, how about that. You want one more fling with Hollis the hottie before you tie the knot. That's it, right?" He smoothed back his hair and winked.

"Huh? What? Ewwww, no. Are you out of your ever-lovin' mind? Not *that* kind of proposition." I stifled a gag. This was not the way to talk if I wanted Hollis to agree to my great plan. I took a deep breath. "Look, I have some good news for you."

"Your bed or mine?"

Lord have mercy and keep me from strangling the man with my bare hands! "Just listen to me for a change. Once upon a time your great- great-who-knows-how-many greats grandfather Beaumont won Rosegate in a card game from Thaddeus Vanderpool. Cornelius McGuire, that auction guy, found the deed and with you being the last of the Beaumonts, you're legally entitled to Rosegate. But I'm here to give you Cherry House instead. You've always wanted Cherry House."

Hollis spilled wine down the front of his shirt and didn't even notice.

"This happened about a hundred and thirty years ago," I rushed on while the gods of dumbstruck were with me. "I just found out tonight, and here's the deal: I know you think Rosegate is a Savannah jewel, and Cherry House is a swine's ear, but Cherry House is perfect now. It's completely renovated, expanded to three floors, and with your dad bequeathing your family home to the city as the Beaumont Museum, this gives you a fine, old house of your own *if* you make the swap tonight. My Prissy Fox Consignment Shop is on the first floor. With your wife's new event planning business set there, Lou Ella could do even better than she is now. The zoning is already in place, and there's parking in the alley. You owe me, Hollis. I found the killer when you were accused of murdering Cupcake and your sorry behind was rotting in jail and--"

"Cherry House?" Hollis babbled.

"The deed to Rosegate will be tied up for years in court. You'll look like a creep for tossing KiKi Vanderpool who taught half the citizens of this fair city to dance and Doc Putter who saved even more from butter-induced cholesterol overload out of their beloved house. And think of this: if you take Putter's and KiKi's house you'll be an outcast, a pariah. You'll never get invited to any social functions of note in Savannah again. You know how Lou Ella enjoys the social standing of being a

Savannah Beaumont." The main reason she married Hollis in the first place if you asked me.

"I have to decide now?"

"If McBride announces it first, he grabs the headline. If you make it public, you're a hero. It will look as if you found out and made the selfless decision."

"Hero?"

"A tribute to the Beaumont family name."

"Lou Ella does want to attract the high-end events. That's where the real money is." Hollis stroked his chin, a sly grin spreading across his lips. "Oh, this is good, really good, she can support me. I can give up the real estate business and be a man of leisure. I can go fishing. I got my eye on this sweet little forty-two-footer over on Whitemarsh Marina."

And there in a nutshell was why Hollis Beaumont was indeed my ex. The man had three real loves in his life: me, myself and I. "First thing tomorrow, contact the press. Say you found out about Rosegate, but the bet happened a long time ago and out of respect for the Vanderpools and blah, blah, blah. When Boone and I get back from our honeymoon, things will have died down. You and Lou Ella move into Cherry House and Walker and I move to his house. It'll look like a final divorce settlement between us now that I'm remarrying. And best of all, you're the hero."

Hollis beamed. "That should earn me an invite to the Telfair Museum Christmas Ball this year for sure, and with a little luck Lou Ella will be planning it all. I'll need a new tux, something with a cummerbund. I got a thing for cummerbunds." He patted his expanding middle, then his brows narrowed. "How can I trust you?"

I knelt down, dumped the contents of Old Yeller out on the stoop and rooted through two lipsticks, a brush with sparkles on the handle, flashlight, flip cell phone, two chew toys.

"Aren't you afraid of toxic waste from that thing?"

I stuck my tongue out at Hollis and retrieved a receipt from Cakery Bakery and my pen with the pink pompom on the end. I was no lawyer but something handwritten, dated, and signed usually held up in court. "Here." I handed him the receipt.

"Two sprinkle doughnuts and two coffees."

"Other side." I passed him the pen.

Hollis held the receipt to the porch light. "It says I give up all rights to Rosegate and you agree to give me Cherry House in two weeks, free and clear." He snorted. "Looks good to me. Are you sure you don't want to seal this deal with a little hanky-panky? I'm feeling pretty frisky right now. I could do with some hanky-panky."

I threw the half-gone box of orange Tic-Tacs at Hollis, BW peed on his foot, and Hollis signed.

It was after midnight when BW and I finally rounded the corner onto Gwinnett. We took the long way home, needing time to process that the house we love, and I affectionately dubbed 'the money-pit,' was no longer ours. I'd opened the Prissy Fox on the first floor to support the house and now it belonged to Hollis. I never imagined this could happen. I intended to stay in Cherry House till they carted me out in a pine box. *Then again, it's like Auntie KiKi says, if you want to make God laugh tell him your plans.*

The porch light to Cherry House was on and the front window of my consignment shop spotlighted Gwendolyn, the mannequin I'd retrieved from a dumpster dive over on Abercorn. I had her dressed in a coral blouse, tan skirt, and a brown leather cross-body bag that would sell in no time.

I passed the gnarled cherry tree that gave the house its name and stopped by the cute little Prissy Fox sign Mamma had made up for me when I opened the shop six years ago. I gazed across the front yard to Rosegate with the living room light still on. Auntie KiKi was awake and no doubt fretting over the blasted deed. Uncle Putter was probably upstairs asleep with head-phones, listening to something like *Sixty-Five Ways to Polish Your Golf Clubs.* In Savannah golf was more religion than sport proven by the fact that Uncle Putter carried a putter everywhere in case a golf ball suddenly dropped to earth and he had to sink a birdie to save the planet.

The thought of not living next to Auntie KiKi and Uncle Putter was a heartbreak, but it beat the heck out of them losing their house. The question was when to tell the big news? Now, and maybe they'd sleep better knowing they'd keep Rosegate? But then Auntie KiKi would throw a hissy and try to talk me out of the swap, and there'd be Savannah-style drama with wailing and crying and maybe even some swooning. I wasn't up for swooning.

Maybe tomorrow after the wedding? I could say something like *Hey, I gave Cherry House to Hollis instead of him taking your house.* Then Boone, BW and I could jump in Boone's red '57 convertible and speed off for our honeymoon on Mackinac Island, and why in the world was a white SUV skidding to a stop at the curb right in front of me?

"This is it!" A gal in skintight jeans, red silk blouse and matching stilettos hopped from the car and flipped back her long red hair. It was Scarlett Rose from *People Want to Know,* a show that dished Savannah dirt. "Get that camera rolling, Delta. This has to be on tonight's news roundup."

Okay, me marrying Boone was definitely an event at least in my book, but breaking TV news? Except it wasn't me Scarlett had in her sights because she ran straight past me, her impos-sibly high heels clacking on the sidewalk as she raced for Rosegate.

Not good. This had Corny McBride written all over it! After his great extortion plan failed and he almost got blasted with a shotgun, my guess was that he downed his weight in booze at a local watering hole and ran his mouth off about the deed. If he couldn't get money from Auntie KiKi, at least he could ruin her reputation?

"Wait." BW and I charged after Scarlett. "Hey, it's late. You can't just barge in on my aunt and uncle."

Scarlett glanced back at me, her cherry-red lips cutting a smirk across her face. "Honey, I'm the press, and I got rights." She parked one hand on her shapely hip and banged on the solid oak door with the other hand. "No use hiding in there, KiKi Vanderpool. We got questions for you that need answering."

"Whatdoyouwant?" Auntie KiKi hissed as she opened the door just a crack. From what I could see, her hair was more bird's nest than coiffure, and she had on an old gray housecoat instead of the lovely purple dress. Her eyes were wild.

"Go away. I didn't do a bloomin' thing. I'm innocent, totally innocent I tell you." She blinked, her eyes clearing.

"You're...you're not the cops?"

Scarlett jabbed a microphone in front of Auntie KiKi, the camera light reflecting off her sweaty forehead. "Scarlett Rose here and people want to know if it's true this house actually belongs to Hollis Beaumont and not the Vanderpools, and it looks like someone shot a big old hole clear through your ceiling. Get a good picture of that hole, Delta. You don't see that every day."

KiKi poked the barrel of the shotgun through the door crack and aimed it at Scarlett. "Like my grandpappy used to say, there's right and there's dead right. What do you have your little old heart set on being tonight?"

I elbowed my way between the shotgun and the microphone

and grinned at the camera. "This is a misunderstanding, and everything is being worked out."

"Not according to Cornelius McGuire." Scarlet gave me a don't-you-dare-argue-with-me glare. "Word has it that after four key lime pie martinis at Jen's and Friends, Mr. McGuire started flashing around an old deed and saying that the Vanderpools have been living in this house that doesn't really belong to them. So, have the Vanderpools taken advantage of the Beaumonts? People want to know if they swindled the Beaumonts out of their rightful home."

"Hollis Beaumont has a home," I said. "And out of respect for the Vanderpools and the fact that the deed transfer happened over a hundred years ago, Mr. Beaumont wants no claim on Rosegate. Go ask him if you don't believe me. He's calling a press conference tomorrow to straighten this all out."

Scarlett's sneer slipped a notch.

"There is no story," I added. "Everyone is happy with the house they have."

Scarlett did another hair toss. "Well, if that don't beat all. The bartender said he had a scoop. This is just a total waste of time." She hooked her arm in the air and started for the van. "Come along, Delta. We got to find another story fast. We're on a deadline here."

Scarlett and crew trotted off and I yanked open the front door. BW and I slid inside. I slammed the door shut behind me and faced Auntie KiKi. "You and your shotgun just might be all over the eleven o'clock news."

"Keeps burglars away."

"Our only hope is for murder and mayhem to descend upon the city and give Scarlett and *People Want to Know* something better to talk about."

Auntie KiKi rested the shotgun against the wall, pushed back a wayward strand of hair and swiped the sweat from her forehead. "Honey, let's do leave out that murder part. You need to be getting yourself home."

"Did you hear what I said to Scarlett about Hollis and that you get to keep Rosegate?"

"What about Rosegate?"

"Have you been hitting Uncle Putter's Scotch?"

"Scotch is fine." Auntie KiKi nibbled her bottom lip, a faraway look in her eyes. "I'm sure everything's fine."

"Nothing's been fine around here for months." I waved my hand in front of her face to get her attention. "Are you listening to me? Why are you in the old housecoat you wear for cleaning out the garage, and there's chocolate on your chin. What happened to that big urn of yellow mums on the entrance table? Why are there pink rose petals on the floor, and where's the hall carpet?"

I started for the ballroom. "Did the florist screw up the flowers? Maybe we should use the sage tablecloth on the cake table instead of a white one and--"

"Forgettheballroom!" Auntie KiKi held my hand in a vise grip and hauled me toward the door with BW getting dragged along. "The flowers are fine, the carpet's fine and the vase got hijacked by the garden fairies." She opened the door, shoved me through, nudged BW with her knee then slammed the door fast, leaving us on the front porch.

"What in the world is going on?" I asked BW.

"What's going on is our wedding." Walker slid his arm around my waist and pulled me close, his chest nestled against my back, his breath hot against my neck. "I saw the TV truck. Scarlett Rose is ten miles of bad road. She makes up stories even when there aren't any. My guess is she got wind of the Rosegate deed."

"Hollis took the swap, so all is well. But the weirdest thing is just now when I told Auntie KiKi she got to keep Rosegate, she didn't bat an eye." I turned to face Boone. "After months of going bonkers and nearly blowing Corny to kingdom come, you'd think she'd be doing cartwheels on the front lawn that she gets to stay in her house."

Boone nibbled my ear. "Maybe she's relieved at a happy ending." He gave me a soft kiss. "And happy about us. It's a miracle we wound up together. I did represent Hollis in your divorce."

I wrapped my arms around Boone's neck. "And I broke into your office, stole your gun, and shot a hole in the wall."

"Yeah, but you didn't shoot a hole in me. I think we first got together when I drove you and BW to the vet when he ate the chocolate."

"And then you caught KiKi when she fell off the fire escape. That made you the family hero." I ran my hands though Boone's thick, dark hair. "It made you my hero." I kissed Boone's very kissable lips. "You make me happier than I ever imagined I could be. You make me feel loved. You make me feel cherished. In fact," I cleared my throat and framed his handsome face in my hands, "from now on I, Reagan Gloria Summerside, promise with all my heart to be yours, Walker J. Boone. I promise to be with you in good times when the sun is shining, and when things go right to hell, which happens a lot around here. I'll be beside you in sickness and in health, through our successes and our total flops. I promise to create wonderful memories with you and BW, and I will walk beside you forever and ever. You, are the absolute love of my life."

Boone grinned and tucked a strand of hair behind my ear. "Uh, I think you're supposed to be saying that to me tomorrow in front of a bunch of people."

"It's better now with only the three of us huddled together out here on this beautiful fall evening, with a full harvest moon overhead, and a sky filled with stars." I gave a little shrug.

"Besides, I just couldn't wait."

"Well, since you started it..." Boone kissed the tip of my nose, his black eyes peering deep into mine as he held me tighter. "Reagan Summerside, I love you for the terrific person you are and who I am when I am with you. You make me want to do better, be better. From this moment on I promise to join my life with yours. Wherever you and BW go, Sweething, I'm going too. Whatever you face, we'll face it together. I'll feed you peppermint tea when you're sick and hold you when you're sad. I'm yours forever because I can't imagine life without you. You are my beautiful, unpredictable, at times hair-raising partner, and I will always have your back no matter what."

"Really?"

"Really."

"All that?"

"And so much more."

"I love you, Walker Boone."

"Right back at you, Sweething."

CHAPTER 3

Candles flickered merrily, and the scent of flowers filled the room. Next-door neighbors, Elsie and Annie Fritz, crooned on about it being a wonderful world, and fifty guests sat waiting for me to walk down the aisle and marry the man of my dreams. After all the crazy with Corny, I didn't dare hope things could be perfect...but, miracle of miracles...today they were.

"How do we go about getting this here shindig over by eleven?" Auntie KiKi whispered as we gazed at my three besties starting down the aisle in front of us and heading toward Mamma, who stood under the rose arch.

"Huh?" I gulped, feeling a little of my perfect day wobble. I kept the happy-bride smile plastered on my face and held tight to a bouquet of yellow mums and white roses. "We got Rosegate back. Boone's in a tux, for crying out loud. I can actually fit in this dress, and you want it all over with? Do you have any idea what it took to get Big Joey, grand poo-bah of the Seventeenth Street Gang, as best man *and* to wear a bowtie? Naming our first-born after him was mentioned if there is a first born. And isn't BW just adorable carrying the ring basket? You've been out in left field all day, and nearly had an aneurism when I wanted to move the cake table."

"That table is fine where it is. This all needs to end in six hours flat, or there will be hell to pay and then some." Auntie KiKi grabbed my arm and I gave thanks to the wedding gods that I had on sneakers and not six-inch heels as she trotted me down the aisle.

"Hey, slow down," Boone said in a laughing whisper. He took my hands in his. "I'm not going anywhere."

"Something's up with Auntie KiKi."

"That's like saying the sky's blue and water's wet, and besides, it can't be as interesting as what's going on right up here." Boone's eyes twinkled and he kissed me on the cheek.

"Hey, you two." Mamma wagged her finger. "None of that till the end." Everyone laughed, and Mamma started in with "Today is a true celebration of us all here together. It's a celebration of love, of deep unfailing friendships, of family, and most of all, it's a celebration of commitment of two people--and dog--in love and who are in this marriage forever."

Boone recited his vows from last night, and I did the same. BW didn't eat the rings, a bit of a worry since I slid them onto a carrot so they wouldn't get lost. Had I used a hotdog, this would have been a ringless wedding and future days of sifting through...well you get the picture.

"Girlfriend," Mercedes giggled as she swished up next to Boone and me after the ceremony and dinner. "That pot roast was plum fantastic, and I told you these here fuchsia dresses would be a crowd pleaser." Mercedes did a twirl, looking like cotton candy caught in a windstorm. "Everyone's going on and on about 'em"

For better or worse, that part was true enough. The choice of color had nothing to do with my love of purple/pink and every-thing to do with it being a bribe when I needed Mercedes to help me hijack a body from the House of Eternal Slumber, where she happened to be a mortician beautician. Everyone needs a BFF with special talents, even if they had questionable taste in bridesmaid dresses.

"It's time to cut the cake," Auntie Kiki announced after tapping her champagne glass to get everyone's attention. She snagged Boone's arm, then mine, and hustled us toward the cake table. "By my calculations," she whispered, "we have thirty-two minutes to eat cake."

"What calculations?" I asked.

"Two hours and thirty-six minutes of dancing," she went on, "and then, I'm turning out the lights and everybody skedaddles out of here. Got it." Auntie KiKi added an evil eye squint to underline her words. No one argued with Auntie KiKi's eye squint, even on their wedding day.

"KiKi really *is* having a meltdown," Boone said to me while we stood hip-to-hip and cut the first slice of red velvet cake decked out in delish buttercream icing. "Think it's stress?"

"I think it's best we don't know." The camera gal flashed pictures as Boone fed me a bite, and I returned the favor. We both shared a sliver with BW, then the DJ played "Sugar, Sugar" while we passed out cake, giving us a chance to mix and mingle. Elvis warbled "Can't Help Falling in Love With You," and Boone waltzed me around the room in our first official dance.

"Okay," I said, releasing a pent-up breath while adding a twirl. "Everything's fine for real, right? No Corny, no Scarlett Rose, no new holes in the hall ceiling."

The guests joined the dancing in the little ballroom filled with soft candlelight, happy times, and wonderful memories. Mamma looked radiant as Swain glided her across the floor. Big Joey did some fancy two-stepping with Earlene, his on-again off-again flame and resident bus driver. Pillsbury, the *dough boy* for the Seventeenth Street Gang who minded the books, danced with Chantilly, the best caterer on the planet. Auntie KiKi looked as if she hadn't slept in weeks.

Boone took me in a wide spin, letting my lovely dress flow out behind me like a soft cloud, then he dipped me just like we'd practiced. I laughed, feeling the tension of the day fade away until I spied something sparkling under the cake table. "Do that dip thing again."

Boone leaned me back.

"Farther."

"That would be a headstand."

I arched a little more to get a better look, hoping I didn't see what I thought I saw, until my trusty sneakers slipped on a dab of dropped icing. I bumped against the cake table, sending it backwards. My stomach did a double flip, with my heart squeezing so tight I thought my eyes would pop out. Everyone laughed. Boone and I stopped and stared at the wedge of floor between us.

"Tell me that's not an arm," Boone whispered from the corner of his mouth.

"Let's go with tweed sleeve." I did a quick dance step to kick it under the table, but it plopped back out. This time a hand was attached with a gold signet ring, catching the light. "What do we do now?"

"Now," Coroner Carver said as he snagged me around the waist and flashed a whitening-strip smile, "it's my turn to dance with the bride. I've waited all night for this and can't wait another minute."

I fluffed my dress over the appendage and Carver added, "They call me Twinkle Toes down at the morgue." Carver dragged me and my puffy dress onto the dance floor, leaving the arm-plus-hand-plus-ring right out there in the open for all to see. Boone and I exchanged *holy freaking cow* looks.

Mercedes blurted, "Why I do declare, I think someone's had a bit too much of the bubbly and done passed out."

Mercedes trotted over to the arm and toed it with the tip of her gold shoe. "Get up, honey. The night's still young. We're just getting started around here."

The arm flopped back to the floor with a dull, solid, lifeless thud.

Mercedes sucked in a quick breath. "Or maybe not?"

Annie Fritz screamed; sister Elsie fainted; Twinkle Toes whipped out his undertaker business card; and Uncle Putter started for the table. "I Want to Hold Your Hand" suddenly blared from the DJs station. My once-upon-a-time perfect wedding day slid right down the drain.

"Stop!" Aldeen Ross bellowed in her I-am-the-police voice that +she used so expertly when not being my maid of honor. "Nobody moves a muscle."

Music ceased, and Aldeen gathered up the folds of her bridesmaid dress and elbowed her way to the arm. She tossed back the tablecloth with a flourish, revealing Corny: face up, eyes vacant, toupee drooped over his ear, and head bashed in on one side.

Uncle Putter felt for a pulse then draped a napkin over Corny's face, indicating that he wasn't about to join the wedding festivities anytime soon.

Aldeen pinched the bridge of her nose and sighed. "Can we not, for the love of all that's holy, get through one little old wedding around here without stumbling across a corpse?"

"I'll have you know," I huffed, feeling the need to defend myself and my recent propensity for finding dead bodies, "I've personally been corpseless for one hundred eighty-four days...not that I've been counting."

"Well, bless my heart." Auntie KiKi tisked from the far side of the ballroom. All eyes turned in her direction as she clasped her hands to her chest. "What in the world is Cornelius McBride doing under the cake table, of all places?"

"Maybe he was looking for your hat." Aldeen pointed. "The one lying right next to him on this rug, that I do believe belongs in your hallway? This *is* the hat I saw you wearing last night at the rehearsal dinner, is it not? Minus the cat fur, of course."

"Maybe." Auntie KiKi put her hands on her hips. "But Corny had it coming. We all know that man is after things that don't belong to him. And I'll tell you something else, if he had his way, Putter and I would be living over at the Hampton Inn and Hollis Beaumont the Third would be moving himself in here lock, stock, and barrel. But now..." A sly smile tripped across Auntie KiKi's lips. "Why, it seems that fate has intervened, and Corny McBride's gotten his comeuppance. It's to my credit I didn't do the old boy in myself, and it wasn't for lack of trying. Last night, I introduced him to the business end of Great-Granddaddy Vanderpool's shotgun and ended up blasting a hole in my ceiling. It wasn't from a water leak like I told you all, but-"

"But nothing more." Mamma clamped her hand over Auntie KiKi's mouth while she mumbled on about finding Corny on the "call tar pit" ...or maybe that was "hall carpet."

Aldeen Ross wagged her head. "I can't believe I'm doing this."

"Wearing a fuchsia bridesmaid dress and looking at a dead person at a wedding?" I said hopefully. "Auntie KiKi said she didn't do it," I pleaded.

"Like I haven't heard that one before. KiKi Vanderpool you are under arrest for the murder of Cornelius McBride."

"I should get a pedal. The rumbag had it humming," Auntie KiKi mumbled under Mamma's hand.

Aldeen slid handcuffs from the bodice of her bridesmaid dress and snapped them over KiKi's wrist. I wasn't sure which astounded me more: that my auntie was under arrest at my wedding or that Aldeen Ross had cuffs stuffed in her bra. Back in the day, when being well-endowed was more dream than fact, I did the Kleenex thing. Handcuffs

was a new one.

"You hold down the fort," Boone said to me, dragging me out of the wedding-day-from-hell trance. "I'll go with Putter and KiKi to the police station and see what I can do about bail."

Sirens sounded in the distance, and I blinked a few times, trying to get my brain working. "But...but you're in a tux."

Boone grinned. "Not by choice."

"You're gorgeous. If you go out in public someone's going to take you home and eat you up with a spoon."

Boone's grin widened. "There's only one home I'm interested in."

He started off and I snagged his arm. "What can I do?"

"Take care of the guests. I suggest an abundance of alcohol and very tall glasses and, oh yeah." Boone kissed me hard and added a wink. "Find a spoon."

CHAPTER 4

Moonlight danced across my front yard and the last of the police cruisers and neighborhood gawkers faded off into the night. Mamma took a gulp straight out of the champagne bottle, and BW and I sat on my front porch, waiting for Boone and hopefully Auntie KiKi and Uncle Putter to show. Mamma swiped her mouth with the back of her hand. She let out a very unjudgelike burp and passed me the bottle. "Honey, here's the thing...some days you get the bear, and some days he just up and eats you hook, line, and sinker."

I nodded in agreement because somehow in my present state of numbness, what Mamma said made perfect sense. I took a swig and passed back the bottle. BW snuggled closer to fight off the late night...or was it early morning now...chill. I burrowed into my old yellow fleece that didn't exactly go with my wedding dress, flowing out across the steps.

"Well, the ceremony was lovely," I added, trying to cheer us up. "And the cake was terrific, and the music was pretty good."

"Yep." Mamma hiccupped. "It was all picture-perfect until that arm slid out from under the table and stole the show. Ya know, I get that sister dear had it in for Corny and that she'd hide the body and not go ruining your wedding. But head-bashing certainly isn't her style, especially when you consider there's a perfectly good shotgun mounted above the fireplace."

Quiet settled in around us, and Mamma passed the bottle. "So, I suppose the real question we have to consider is, who else besides KiKi wanted Corny's change-of-address card to read Bonaventura Cemetery?"

"And who wanted to frame Auntie KiKi for the deed?" I added.

"And," Boone chimed in as he rounded the side of the house and strolled up the walkway from the garage, waving a yellow Post-it, "who slipped Cornelius McBride this note?"

Boone's hair was mussed, tie loose at his neck, tux jacket slung over his shoulder and--thank you, Jesus--he was all mine. "I couldn't get KiKi bailed out," Boone said. "Nothing gets done on the weekends in lockup, but it just so happens that Putter did triple bypass on the desk sergeant's brother. When I left, Grubhub had just delivered a pepperoni pizza, KiKi was sitting in a recliner with a martini in hand, and Putter was watching *Fairway to Heaven* on ESPN. Never underestimate the powers of a Southern belle and a good heart surgeon."

"What's this about a note?" Mamma asked.

Boone handed her the paper. She held it up to the light spilling out from the front display window and read, *"Changed my mind, you scum bucket. Rosegate at midnight."*

Boone parked down between BW and me. He draped his jacket over BW, slid his arm around my waist and planted a soft kiss on my cheek. "Aldeen didn't find Corny's phone but she did discover the note in Corny's jacket pocket. The original was written on a Jen's and Friends napkin and the lab is checking for fingerprints. I think Aldeen gave me the info because she felt bad that I was at the police station instead of on my honeymoon."

"Or she wanted you to go fishing around, figuring you'd get better answers than the police," I said. "When Auntie KiKi left here last night, she was probably headed off to Jen's and Friends. Scarlett Rose said Corny was there. Anyone could have seen Auntie KiKi, heard Corny blathering on about Rosegate and used the opportunity to lure Corny to Rosegate, knock him off and frame KiKi."

"Any five-year-old with a Popsicle stick can jimmy those old windows at Rosegate." Mamma added another hiccup. "With the wedding and delivering flowers and setting up chairs and tables, KiKi kept the place unlocked half the time anyway. Could be that we're looking for someone who has it in for KiKi and Corny. Someone who wants to pick off two stones with one bird."

Mamma stood, swayed a bit then straightened her still-pristine suit. No wrinkle would dare to muss Judge Gloria Summerside, even if she was a wee bit wasted. "This can all wait till tomorrow. I'm tired to the bone. Everett just texted that he's on his way to ferry me home, fearing I'm in no shape to be driving. The man knows me pretty well, he does."

Mamma patted Boone's cheek and handed him the champagne bottle. "Remember, this here is your wedding night. Do the Seventeenth Street Gang proud, my dear."

Mamma added a sassy grin then sashayed her way to the curb as a black Caddy rolled up. In spite of everything, Mamma looked happy, and who knew the woman could sashay?

"Not exactly the night we planned," Boone said to me. "We'll make up for it later."

I scooted onto Boone's lap and nibbled his bottom lip. "Forget later." I reached into my jacket pocket and slid out a silver spoon. "This night's not over yet."

. . .

BW AND I WALKED INTO THE JAIL CELL EARLY THE NEXT MORNING and were greeted by "Woe is me," from Auntie KiKi. Actually, it wasn't all that early, more like noon, but you got to cut a girl some slack after her wedding night.

"Woe? What woe?" I took in the circumstances. "You're sitting at a cherry table and dining on biscuits and gravy. Is that Spode china? You're supposed to be eating gruel off a tin try and worried to a frazzle you'll end up in the clink for the rest of your natural days."

"Oh, for pity's sake, does anyone even know what gruel is?" KiKi added a dollop of gravy to her biscuit. "And this truly is a woeful time if you think about it. All the chicken gravy is gone, and I'm stuck here with cream gravy. And as for frazzled, it's like Cher says: 'If you really want something, you can figure out how to make it happen.' I'm leaving that figuring part up to you and Walker."

Back in the day Auntie KiKi was a roadie for Cher, never quite left the tour, and she never let us forget it. Today, she had on a pink warm-up suit, dangle earrings, and her auburn hair frizzed out under a headband. Cher would have been proud. I took the chair across from Auntie and snagged a perfect biscuit before she polished them off. "Tell me exactly what happened at Jen's and Friends," I said around a mouthful.

"The Snickers martini was sublime."

"I mean like who was there." I fed BW a chunk of biscuit then licked a blob of gravy off my thumb. "The police found a note in Corny's jacket pocket saying you'd changed your mind and he should meet you at Rosegate. Mamma, Boone and I think the killer saw you downing martinis then slipped Corny the note to lure him to Rosegate."

Auntie KiKi stopped her teacup midair. "Uh oh. I forgot all about the blasted note."

This time my teacup froze midair and my heart stopped dead in my chest. "Define 'blasted.'"

"On a Jen's and Friend's napkin, printed with my new eyebrow pencil that I'd picked up at Sephora for the wedding. Kiss of Honey it was, and now that I think about it, that's not the right shade for me at all. Too dark, makes me look like I'm getting ready to hold up the local 7-Eleven and--"

I snagged the cup from Auntie KiKi's hand, sloshing tea on the little table. I leaned across and looked her dead in the eyes and whispered through clenched teeth, "Why didn't you get the note out of Corny's pocket when he was sprawled across your hall carpet?"

Auntie KiKi narrowed her eyes. "If you must know, Miss Smarty Pants, I didn't plan on anyone finding the body under my table. It all started Friday night when I was sitting at Jen's and Friends, having a drink with the gang from Sleepy Pines. Zelda told me that Mildred Heatherweight got rushed to the hospital earlier with chest pains, and that life was too short to be having all this stress over Corny and Rosegate. She said I should just pay Corny off and be done with it. I didn't have a better idea, so I wrote Corny the note to meet up. The next thing I know, I'm wrapping Corny's bony carcass in my hall carpet and sliding that piece of scum across my living room floor. Good thing I found that there Snickers to keep up my strength or I never would have made it."

"*You* gave Corny the note?"

"Had one of the waiters do it. Didn't trust myself to not impale the dirtbag with my swizzle stick. After he got the note, Corny up and left. I planned on getting one of those Ubers back to the house, but then I went outside and spotted your mamma cutting across Johnson Square, probably heading on home from her hot date. Deep down, I knew Judge Gloria Summerside would never succumb to paying off the likes of Corny McBride, and neither should I. I crossed the street to Johnson Square and parked down on a bench, figuring Corny would leave Rosegate when I didn't show. Instead, I found him on my hall carpet."

"Did anyone see you?"

"Princess was sitting on Corny's chest, cleaning herself."

"I mean, did anyone see you at the park? How could you do this!"

"It was hard work. I can tell you that. Corny weighs more than you think. Google says a dead person gets downright ripe after twenty-four hours. I was worried sick the whole house would smell like a dumpster right there in the middle of your wedding."

That completely killed my appetite, and I fed the rest of the biscuit to BW. "Your bail hearing's at noon on Monday. Boone's working on some fancy double-talk about you being a pillar of the community, and I don't care what Cher says about things happening if you want them to. If your prints show up on the Jen's and Friends napkin, you're toast."

"We all know Cher's the wisdom of the ages so don't you go ragging on my girl. And as for me being toast, there better be enough marmalade."

I gave KiKi a quick kiss. I thanked the desk sergeant for thinking of BW as a little person in a fur coat and allowing him inside to visit KiKi. I headed out of the police station and into the fall day that would have been even lovelier if I wasn't chasing down another killer. Why me?

Actually, I'd figured out a very logical reason behind the *why me*. When Hollis and I divorced, it took one lifeless piece of crud out of my life. The universe figured it had to fill the void and return balance by me finding other lifeless pieces of crud. The good news was that the cruds I found had it coming. The bad news was that I was always caught in the middle.

In the back parking lot, I spied Mamma trying to wedge her

black Caddy...obviously car of choice of Savannah judges...into a parking place suited for a Mack truck. Mamma was many things--insightful judge, wonderful mother, caring sister--but she had scary taste in clothes...thank heavens judges' robes only came in black. And she couldn't drive worth beans, proven by multiple dents and scrapes on her fender and people diving for cover when she barreled down Bull Street toward the courthouse.

"So how is she?" Mamma wanted to know. I ignored the car angled across yellow parking lines. "Is the desk sergeant bonkers yet?"

"He's gone through three packs of gum and pulled out most of his eyebrows. If she doesn't get bail, he'll probably smuggle her out himself. I have news, and not the good kind. Guess who wrote the note found in Corny's pocket then had a WWGD moment and changed her mind?"

Mamma sighed. "I figured as much about the note from the scumbag reference. It's classic KiKi. What in the world is WWGD?"

"*What would Gloria do?* She saw you cutting across the park and had second thoughts about paying up. She knew you wouldn't do it, so neither should she. Anyone might have seen Auntie KiKi in the park. If they knew about the deed and the note, they could have done in Corny and framed her."

I eyed Mamma's new yellow suit that Auntie KiKi insisted she get. "Not typical 'visiting the imprisoned' garb. Meeting a certain love interest?"

"Don't know if I'd jump right to love," Mamma said with a touch of pink in her cheeks. "But there's a whole lot of like going on, that's for sure."

"You're allowed to be happy, even in your--"

"Honey, if you say *in my advancing years, a senior citizen, coffin-dodger, oldster, boomer,* or *scooter-dude* you're out of the will."

"I was going for 'a lovely women in her prime.'" I was really going for advancing years.

Mamma continued on her way to the police station with a little spring in her step. BW and I crossed the street and headed for Habersham. Even with the sun shining and lovely breeze, I was too pooped for springing.

"Look pathetic," I whispered to BW. I eyed the big blue hydrocarbon express rounding the far corner. "Limp."

With any luck, Earlene was at the controls since this was her route. Bridesmaid or not, she'd have no qualms about running me over if I wasn't at an officially designated bus stop. A pitiful dog got her attention every time and made her putty in their paws.

"I should have known," Earlene huffed when BW bounded up the steps into the bus. "You went and did a fake job on me, and I went and fell for it. Didn't you know it's bad luck to fake out the bus driver like that on a Sunday morning, especially when she's a touch under the weather from too much celebrating?"

"I'm supposed to be on my honeymoon today. I should be drinking mimosas and eating breakfast in bed. Don't I get a little pity?"

"Not even a smidgen." Earlene readjusted her driver's cap and closed the door. "Start that pity stuff and folks around here think they can just get on and off anytime and anyplace they please. We'd be headed straight for transportation anarchy."

I didn't know how to argue with impending anarchy, so I dropped the fare in the box and grabbed the first seat. Earlene accelerated with a solid *vroom,* and I asked, "Did you and Big Joey have a nice evening, in spite of..."

"Your uninvited guest? Being that it was your wedding, I suppose we all should have been prepared for anything that popped up, or in this case flopped out."

Earlene pulled to the curb and swung open the bus doors to let on passengers. Three people clambered aboard, flashed their frequent flyer cards and shuffled down the aisle. A thirty-something woman cocooned in a massive black cloak complete with hood followed. Not exactly Sunday morning attire, except for the rose in her hair. She paused, stared at me, glared then stopped dead. "How dare you!"

That covered a lot of territory. These last few, slightly bridezilla, months were a bit hectic. I'd done ten rounds with the florist over the wrong wedding bouquet, so this could be someone from the Purple Posy. I'd bought the most voluminous dress on the planet requiring two seamstresses to get the hem right. Or it could be someone from Tux Masters. I'd sent Big Joey there for a fitting and nearly scared the counter girl half to death.

"I'm sorry," I offered, hoping to cover all the bases.

"Sorry? I'm Emmilene McBride, and my wonderful" --a tear trickled down her cheek-- "amazing" --her voice cracked-- "generous, heartfelt, beloved brother is dead because of your aunt. All you can say is sorry! My life is ruined, my dreams are shattered, my best friend and protector is now lying over there at House of Eternal Slumber in the Green Pastures room."

More likely Corny was with Mr. Dying-to-meet-you at the morgue, but I wasn't about to offer the correction.

Emmilene burst into tears and blubbered, "KiKi Vanderpool killed my Corny. He had the goods on her. She knew it so she killed him dead." Her brows knitted together in one long, angry line. "I know your type all too well. You and your aunt are those richy-bitchy women who put on a big show then go with cheap mums for a wedding. You think you can get away with anything. Well, this time it won't work." Emmilene pointed a bony finger at me. "A plague on both your houses."

The woman buried her face in her hands and let out an ear-piercing wail that sent shivers down my spine and warranted a howl from BW. She folded into her cape like a big bat, and I reached to steady her. Two ladies rushed forward, gave me an eat-dirt-and-die look and guided Emmilene to a seat.

"Maybe you should get off right here," Earlene whispered, "before you cause any more trouble. Emmilene owns Glorious Gardens and is working right hard to make a go of it. We run a stress-free transportation service, and you're upsetting everyone."

"Me? I didn't do anything, and Auntie KiKi's innocent." I said the last part loud enough for everyone to hear. "And she is not a bitchy woman. She's a true Southern lady,"-*most of the time*-"and she's being framed, and I intend to prove it."

Emmilene wailed louder, twenty pairs of condemning eyes glared my way, and Earlene hitched her head toward the still-open door. BW and I did a quick exit and watched the bus pull away in a cloud of exhaust. I caught a glimpse of Emmilene snuggled forlornly in her cape that I actually recognized. Maybe I'd sold it at my shop? Maybe trick-or-treaters? Maybe it was from *Sex It Up* over on Abercorn where I'd picked up a pink boa and stilettos for Boone...not that he'd be the one wearing them. Emmilene huddled close to the window, phone in hand and texting up a storm. I guess no one's ever too distraught to text.

"Well," I said to BW, "that was as depressing as my senior prom date with Henry Winters and his mother. I'm about a quart low on caffeine and feel a two-doughnut day coming on to cheer us up."

BW and I turned up Whittaker along with the one-way traffic inching around Chippewa Square. We hung a right on West Broughton. The green Cakery Bakery awning fluttered up ahead, and I caught a whiff of fat and sugar with a hint of vanilla and cinnamon. I passed tables and chairs clustered on the side-walk for outside pastry consumption, then opened the half-glass, half-wood door. The newly pimped-out Cakery all done up in pinks and soft green was hopping with customers picking up rolls and cakes and pies for Sunday dinner. Being seasoned Cakery Bakery patrons, BW and I hunted for an opening and slithered our way through to the counter.

"The usual?" GracieAnn asked. Without waiting for an answer, she reached around a gal in a pink apron and sailor hat and plucked two sprinkle doughnuts from the display case. "I'm adding a third for Walker," GracieAnn said while slipping the goodies into a pink bag. "Blueberry, lemon yogurt and they're downright healthy. You should give 'em a try." She added a wink, knowing that the idea of abandoning my beloved sprinkles for yogurt was downright laughable.

GracieAnn was about my age, gone pleasantly to plump as all pastry shop owners should, and when she got to heaven the Lord himself would welcome her into his kitchen. "Everyone agreed the wedding cake was to die for," I said to GracieAnn, then added a gulp. "I can't believe I said that."

GracieAnn poured a cup of coffee. "Since it was your wedding, we all should have suspected there'd be a body in the mix somewhere."

"You're the second person to say that to me today."

"And the day's not over. You do have a reputation." GracieAnn rang up the sale then passed over the coffee and doughnuts. "Your unexpected wedding guest had a reputation problem too. Not everyone's crying a river this morning that you-know-who is not walking the streets of Savannah. Take a look."

GracieAnn nodded to the end of the counter and a chocolate cake. It had a little blue fondant coffin next to the words *Never RIP* scripted in white.

"And of course, it's devil's food," GracieAnn added. "Those

seniors at the Pines may not be as spry as they once were, but they sure enough got themselves one wicked sense of humor."

"Sleepy Pines?" That perked me up and I hadn't even had the coffee. The Piners were with Auntie KiKi at Jen's and Friends. From the looks of that cake, some of them truly didn't care for Corny any more than KiKi.

"I can see that you're really swamped. Want me to deliver the cake for you?"

"Aren't you supposed to be on your honeymoon?"

I fed BW a chunk of sprinkle doughnut and stuffed the rest into my mouth, looking a bit like a squirrel storing food for winter. Balancing the cake box, coffee, and pink bag, I wiggled my way back through the throng. Once outside, I set the box on a table. I pulled out my economical, no-frills, cheap-as-all-get-out-so-I-could-afford-it, flip phone then texted Boone for a ride.

When he pulled to the curb, I noticed my new husband looked as tired as I felt. Wedding nights should definitely not be followed by a day of *who did in the dead guy*. BW hopped into the back of the convertible, and I took passenger and held the cake on my lap. Putting cake and dog in the same area was simply too much canine temptation, not to mention that chocolate was a huge no-no, even if BW didn't see it that way.

Boone eyed the cake-with-coffin then eased out into the traffic. "Usually there are candles on a cake. Then again, this is Savannah."

"Sleepy Pines residents are celebrating the demise of our favorite auctioneer." I handed Boone the rest of my coffee and told him about KiKi writing the note and the Piners being at the bar.

"Corny's no saint," Boone said. I took back the coffee and exchanged it for the yogurt doughnut. "But what do the seniors have against KiKi? She's on the board for parks and two hospitals, and even has that Dancing Queen daylily named after her. Kiki's the Betty White of Savannah."

"She stayed at the Pines for that week during our last caper and stirred things up a bit. She won the tango competition and aced out Mildred Heatherweight in a canasta tournament. For the talent show, she did her *Turn Back Time* routine, complete with red boa and black silk dress while perched atop the baby grand. Always a hit with the men."

"Framing her for murder for being a flirt seems a bit much." Boone stopped for a light, a smile playing across his face. "You know, for the rest of that coffee I'd be willing to chat up the ladies at the Pines to see what's what."

I handed Boone the coffee, and we rounded the corner to Orleans Square. The urn fountain dripped lazily in the afternoon sun, strollers wandered about, and Emmilene stood in the middle of a small group of sightseers. I smacked my hand to my forehead. I recognized the cloak, and it had nothing at all to do with *Sex It Up*.

CHAPTER 5

"What?" Boone asked. "Sudden headache?"

"Sudden revelation. That woman in the black cloak by the fountain is Emmilene McBride, Corny's sister. My guess is that she does Savannah tours through historical houses. I did the same thing for extra cash when getting the Fox up and running, and the outfit always got me more customers and bigger tips. She's probably getting ready for an afternoon walk through the Harper Fowlkes House across the street."

I pointed to a Greek revival with transom windows over the front doorway, big columns, and an iron gate in front. "Day tours there aren't so bad, but nights..." I felt a sudden shiver. "The lights are glitchy. On one of my night tours, a guy got separated from the group. When the lights came back on, I found him locked in the upstairs bedroom, mumbling gibberish."

"Big Joey won't even walk past the place after midnight."

The saying goes, if you don't believe in ghosts when you come to Savannah, you sure as heck will when you leave. "Emmilene met up with me on the bus this morning. She blames Auntie KiKi for Corny's demise, and she wished a plague

on both our houses. Not sure what that's all about, but it gave me
the creeps. She must be hard up for cash if she's working the day
after her brother died."

"The plague thing is Romeo and Juliet, and right now, most
of the city blames KiKi for Corny's death."

"You know Shakespeare?"

"Sweething, every man has a bit of Romeo in 'em, and I'll tell
you all about it tonight." Boone added a devil laugh, and we
pulled into the back lot of Sleepy Pines.

BW hopped out of the Chevy, and Boone and I followed with
cake in hand. Leaves somersaulted across the grass, and we cut
through the azaleas and opened the white gate leading to a
stone patio. Today, it was bedecked with yellow tables, green
chairs, and striped umbrellas. Seniors sat about doing the casual
afternoon snack thing and enjoying the weather.

The Pines was a converted old Victorian with wide porches,
big windows and working shutters, and surrounded by a
mismatched fence. The place was resident-owned co-op style,
and most had lived their whole lives here in Savannah. They'd
partied together, argued together and complained about poli-
tics, football, kids, and those rotten Yankees. Nothing much had
changed except their address, the number of candles on
birthday cakes, more trips to the bathroom at night...and that
bowl of potato chips flying through the air, missing me by a hair
and smashing against the stones!

"Dagnabbit, Enos!" bellowed a bald man with enough wrin-
kles to do a roadmap proud. "You're always shooting off your
mouth when you don't know what you're talking about. My
Corny, God rest his soul, was a fine southern gentleman. None
better on this here earth, so you better shut your yap before I
shut it for you."

"You got blinders on, JerryLee," a man with more hair in his
ears than on his head yelled back. "Just because Corny was your

cousin, you think he's lily pure. Well, he's not by a long shot. None of us around here are going to miss Corny McBride one lick. Fact is, most of us think he got what was coming to him. Hell's bells, you had him sell that mahogany sideboard for you, and he didn't get near what it was worth. Margaret Ann got ripped off something fierce with her Biedermeier writing desk."

"The man has to make some commission." JerryLee held up his glass in salute. "To Corny McBride. He saved me from paying senior care taxes by buying my house outright. Bet you didn't get help like that from any of your family. It's just like those government bastards to take every last penny we make."

"Hey, you, over there." Enos pointed his gold-handled cane at Boone. "You're a lawyer. Tell this here old fart there's no such thing as senior taxes, and that his crooked-as-a-dog's-hind-leg cousin done messed him over."

JerryLee wobbled to a standing position. He poised his walker ready for attack, and Enos turned his cane on JerryLee. I held up the Cakery Bakery box and called out the most beloved words of seniors everywhere. "Time for cake."

I wasn't sure how this particular cake would go over with JerryLee, but I'd give him an end piece, and he'd never know about the fondant coffin. Boone hunted plates while I cut slices, and--just like that--peace, harmony, and Southern hospitality returned to Savannah.

"So," I said to Enos as we all dug in and I changed the subject, "these are lovely flowers in the middle of the table."

"Glorious Gardens bring 'em fresh every week, and Corny's a lying, swindling no-good, and I don't care what JerryLee says."

"I heard that," JerryLee muttered from the next table where he sat beside Boone, "and it's not true. Not one rotten word."

A lady next to me, in a flowered dress, lowered her voice and said, "I had an antique silver tea set as part of my estate and appraised at a pretty penny. Corny said he only got a couple hundred for the lot, and I know that was a lie. He did the same shenanigans to Zadie."

Enos jabbed his fork toward a lady with purple hair, a purple jogging suit, and purple sneakers sitting beside Boone. Was she batting her eyes at Boone? Did she just pinch his butt! I started to say, *hey, that's my butt,* but Enos continued on. "Before I had my stroke and came here to live, Zadie gave her coin collection to Captain Swindle for appraisal. When she got it back, the 1943 Lincoln-head penny was gone. 'Course Corny said he never had it in the first place. If Zadie said she gave Corny the whole collection, I believe her. That gal's sharp as a tack. She used to be one of them actuaries who dealt with risk management. She knows her numbers all right. She keeps perfect account of our canasta and gin rummy scores. She even makes our investments and minds our BFF fund."

"Best Friends Forever?"

"Boozy Friday Friends. We get one of them Ubers and pile in, and we head off to Jen's and Friends. We even take JerryLee and all his crankiness and Jeb Wilcox and his wheelchair. Poor devil got mowed down right here in front of this place. With the chair and JerryLee's walker, there isn't much room left in the Uber, so I drive Rocket Man."

Enos nodded to the corner of the patio and a four-wheel red scooter. It had blue racing stripes on the side, white streamers and an American flag off the back.

"My nephew went and souped it up for me." Enos snickered. "He got rid of the speed limiter and added an extra lithium battery. I beat that Uber driver ever time."

Enos thumped his chest like Tarzan. "I know all the back alleys around here and don't get hung up in traffic."

"Is Rocket fast?"

"Is the Pope's Baptist?"

I think Enos got that last part mixed up a little, but God was

God, so close enough. "Can I take Rocket for a spin? I used to have a scooter."

"No one touches Baby."

"How about fifty bucks?"

"Make it a hundred and you got yourself a deal."

Boone was busy with cake, questions, and avoiding Zadie's wandering hands, and as much as Boone belonged to me, I couldn't really blame Zadie for trying. I took the scooter seat and settled in. BW was not one to miss out on a good time, so he wedged himself between my legs and flashed me a happy puppy grin. I turned the key, a low rumble vibrating my butt and up into my spine. I set the speed knob to max to see if Enos had any chance of getting from Jen's and Friends to Rosegate before Corny then bashing him over the head. Gripping the handlebar, I levered the throttle with my thumb, and Baby jumped the curb. We tore across the lawn, plowed through the oleander hedge, knocked the wood pineapple finial off the end of the fence, zoomed onto Tattnall Street, and aced out a Mustang at the stop sign.

Brakes? Sweet Lord above, where were the blasted brakes? I hugged BW between my legs so he wouldn't fly off, dodged oncoming traffic and jerked left. I bumped over the curb into Pulaski Square to avoid more cars and darted around pedestrians. I barely missed two wood benches, swerved around the fountain...Savannah's really big on fountains...and up ahead spotted a wedding?

Seriously? A wedding here *now*! There were rows of white chairs, a white runner with red rose petals and pretty people gathered about. And there was a bride. *Did there have to be a bride right now!*

I cut her off, caught the veil on my shoulders as I clipped the ivy arch and veered around a baby stroller then crashed into a thick row of lilacs that looked amazing in the spring. I toppled onto the grass with BW landing on my chest. Rocket stopped dead, not even breaking a sweat.

"I'm sorry!" I held BW tight, gazed into his terrified brown puppy eyes, and kissed his snout. "I really am! I'm a terrible doggie mommy."

"What in blazes are you doing?" a cop said as he gazed down at me.

"I didn't know where the brake was." I sniffed.

"How could you be so stupid?"

"It takes years of practice." At least that brought a smile.

"I should ticket you for underage driving. You have no business on this scooter. All you had to do was let go of the throttle and the thing stops dead. It's electric powered, not gas."

He tipped back his hat and shook his head. "You're the kind of person who gives seniors a bad rap." The cop yanked the veil off my shoulders. "Get out of here before the bride presses charges."

"Tell her I'm sorry, really sorry." I stood and brushed leaves off BW. I climbed on the death-machine, balanced the dazed pup on my lap, set the speed to low, and put-putted my way to Sleepy Pines.

"What the heck happened?" Boone wanted to know when I climbed out of the cart. "Where did you go? One minute you're eating cake, and the next it's the Indy 500 scooter-style. There's a scratch on your nose, and is that ivy in your hair?" Boone hoisted BW into his arms. "I think you broke our dog."

I plucked a leaf out of my mouth. "Let's just say Enos had no trouble making his way from Jen's and Friends to Rosegate before Corny," I added while we walked to the Chevy. "We know there's no love lost between those two, so that takes care of motive. But it's a big jump from being a conning auctioneer to winding up with a bashed-in head." I slipped into the front seat and held BW on my lap. "Did you find out anything from Zadie and the gang?"

"Zadie needs a hobby."

I kissed Boone on the cheek. "I think she's found one."

We headed for Barnard Street, and Boone said, "I got nothing new on Corny from my table. Mostly there was talk about a Vegas trip paid for by some investment. Caesars Palace has no idea what's headed their way. I can drop you at the jail, but I need to stop at the office and put the polishing touches on the argument to free KiKi. Any ideas what to include?"

"She makes a mean martini?"

Boone stopped for a group of meandering tourists with maps and guidebooks, and I opened the door. "I need to apologize to a certain bride for ruining her wedding with a scooter. What if I pick up conquistador sandwiches for dinner and meet you back at the house?"

"Extra pickles?"

I gave Boone a thumbs-up, and he and a BW drove off. I sidestepped a car going the wrong way around the one-way street and crossed to Pulaski Square. It was one of my faves and named in honor of a truly heroic Revolutionary War general who'd saved Savannah from the Redcoats. Why Pulaski's statue was not in Pulaski Square but two blocks over in Monterey Square was a bit of a mystery. Then again, the statue of James Oglethorpe, Savannah's beloved founding father, was not in Oglethorpe Square but over in Chippewa Square, and William Jasper's monument was in Madison Square. I had no idea where the Madison monument was. Welcome to Savannah.

The wedding party finished up their photoshoot, a lovely sunset blazing behind them. No doubt the guests were already at the reception venue, slurping champagne and downing shrimp cocktails and little tomato sandwiches.

"You!" The bride yelped when she saw me. Oh, Lordy, wasn't

that the same thing Corny's sister bellowed earlier? The bride ran up to me, veil flowing out behind her, bouquet of pink roses and white hydrangeas in hand. She was pretty, young and adorable, and if she punched me, I had it coming.

"I am so, so sorry," I stammered. "I just got married myself-- last night actually--and I know this is such a special day and I ruined it for you. I truly want to apologize for the scooter that I thought I knew how to ride but obviously didn't, and I'm sorry for swiping your veil and for nearly running you over and--"

"You want to apologize?"

"After wedding expenses, I have fifty-three dollars and twenty-six cents in my checking account, so an apology is the best I can do."

"My two best friends got married last month, and their weddings were lovely. All I could imagine for myself today was lovely wedding number three. Who wants to be number three in anything? I had a martini party to kick off the weekend, so that was a bit different, but you and the scooter were the icing on the cake. Now my guests over at the country club are no doubt going on and on about *my* little old wedding. Everyone had their iPhones out, snapping pictures, and I bet I'm on every Instagram account in Savannah. Whose wedding are they going to be talking about forever and ever?" The bride did a little dance and pointed herself in the chest. "Mine!"

"You're...happy?"

"Ecstatic."

Mercedes walked up and the bride plucked a gorgeous pink rose with a touch of yellow from her bouquet and handed it to me. "You earned it. It's a Claude Monet. Isn't it the bomb. That new president of the Savannah Garden Club did all the flowers for my wedding weekend. Emmilene cuts them right out of her very own garden. It's amazing, I've seen pictures. So, tell me about your wedding. Was it lovely or a bit more memorable like mine?"

"We found a dead guy under the cake table."

"Girl, you should franchise!"

The bride scurried back to her new husband, and Mercedes took a sniff of the rose. "What happened to KiKi being president of the Garden Club? Not enough fertilizer in her petunias?"

"Maybe not enough winners in the rose competition. Mrs. Becker came in third, pitched a fit right there in front of the judges and they had to call an ambulance. Pastor Chandler gave her mouth-to-mouth till the paramedics showed up, but he's been wanting to do that for years. Until yesterday Auntie KiKi was still the prezzie. I should warn her that Emmilene's gunning for her job." I held the rose up to the fading sunlight. "I've never seen a rose like this before. Have you over at the Slumber?"

"Honey, I see a whole lot of flowers in ever shape and size in my line of work. They come in the side door, go out the back-door, get tossed into the body buggy along with the dearly departed, and all wind up at the cemetery. Did you ever notice that no one ever sends candy? What naturally goes with flowers? Candy. I could do with a little candy now and then."

I had no comeback to the candy thing, and the body buggy threw me for a loop, so I changed the subject. "I'm headed over to Zunzi's to get a conquistador for Boone. Want to tag along?"

"For Boone?" Mercedes gave me a *yeah, right* eye roll as we stepped around an orange tour trolley with the guide spouting tales of Savannah the beautiful. "We all know you're the conquistador queen around here. They should put your face on their logo like that Wendy's girl or that dude in the white suit selling fried chicken. So, how is married life treating you?"

"Corny's dead. Auntie KiKi's in the slammer. A killer's on the loose, I'm not on my honeymoon, and we got three electric can openers as wedding gifts."

"Your SpaghettiO surprise is legendary, and hey, look, there's one of our delivery people." Mercedes pointed to the front of the Harper Fowler house. "I recognize the outfit. The Slumber gets weird enough with all that low lighting and music to die by going on. Then somebody shows up in a long black cloak with a bunch of flowers and really creeps me out."

"That's Corny's sister. That's Emmilene, the one passing herself off as president of the Garden Club. She won't talk to me with being Auntie KiKi's niece, but you could find out what's going on."

"No way." Mercedes took a step back. "I hate the Fowler house." She held up her fingers making a little cross.

"You could go on one of her tours and get her talking. Just ask a few questions about flowers," I pushed on. "Keep it simple, chatty, mention the Claude Monet rose and the Garden Club and see what she says. Auntie KiKi doesn't need to be blindsided if there's a flower coup and someone's taking over her presidency. She's got enough problems at the moment. Didn't Uncle Putter do that heart valve repair on your cousin last year?"

"I knew I should have just kept on walking, but did I? Nooooo! I had to stop and see what my good pal Reagan, was up to. I was headed to Leapold's for a double dip of peanut butter chippy, and now you want me to go through a haunted house at night?"

"Dusk."

"I hear tell a secret society used to meet in that place since back in the days of George Washington and they haven't all left the party. Sometimes on a moonless night, if you look up there at the third floor, you can see old men floating about in tuxes. You can smell their cigars. They are truly not going to appreciate a woman of my particular complexion breaking up their event. I can tell you that."

"I'll pay for your ticket. You'll be in a group and in and out before any haunting starts. You're used to being around dead people, so what's the big deal?"

"My dead people stay put!"

"There's a conquistador in it for you," I singsonged. "Just think of the crusty French bread, the special sauce in every bite. Imagine licking it off your fingers and some dripping down your arm."

"You don't play fair, you know that?"

"These are desperate times." I handed Mercedes twenty bucks and watched her head on over to Emmilene. For bribery sake and the wellbeing of Auntie KiKi's presidency, thank heavens I wasn't the only conquistador queen in Savannah.

CHAPTER 6

Where in the heck was Mercedes? From my bench behind the fountain in Orleans Square, I kept my gaze fused to the front door of the Harper Fowlkes House. Lights in the square blinked on, and tourists filed out of the grand house and faded into the evening. Couples strolled past me on their way to Rue de Jean or Husk Savannah with the best hearth-baked cornbread on the planet. There was no Mercedes. A house tour and a few innocent questions: What could go wrong with that...asked the girl with the dead guy under the cake table?

Emmilene stood in the main doorway, holding her lantern and backlit by the huge entrance hall chandelier. She bid another couple good-bye and waved them off, and my flip phone rang. Why did that darn thing always have to settle to the bottom of my purse?

"Mercedes?" I said after finding the phone. "Where in blazes are you?"

"Girl, one minute I'm in a closet, admiring an evening gown with seed pearls and silver sequins, and just like that, the door closes behind me and I'm locked in. I tried to find another way out, but this here closet is a bloomin' fortress."

"Emmilene locked you in a closet? What did you do?"

"I did what you said to do. I asked about the rose, and I mentioned the bouquet. Then she asked if I was getting married. That got me flustered 'cause it got me thinking about my man, Pillsbury. I happened to mention you just got married. She told me to mind my own business or else, then I got locked in the closet. There's ten percent left on my phone before the flashlight dies, and it's dark as the devil's dishrag in here. Just so you know, if I start smelling cigar smoke, I'm screaming the place down."

I needed a distraction. No way would Emmilene let me in the house. First step was to get her away from the front door. I searched through the numbers I had stored in old Flippy and found the one for Harper Fowlkes, from when I did tours. It was closing time, but depending on Emmilene's present financial situation, the prospect of a good-tipping customer reserving a few spots for tomorrow's tour might be enough of an enticement to take the call.

I crossed the street and hunkered down behind the boxwood bushes in front of the wrought-iron fence. I said a little prayer there were no creepy crawlies or—even worse—snakes, since October was one of their favorite months to slither about looking for a place to winter.

Emmilene wouldn't take the call when my name showed up on caller ID, so I used a slick little trick Big Joey showed me. Hit 67, put in the number, hit Call, and bingo the call goes through with no ID. I could hear ringing through the open front door and crossed my fingers I did the trick right.

Looking irritated, Emmilene folded her arms, unfolded them, stomped her foot, then ducked inside. Keeping to the shadows, I tippy-toed up the front steps and around the big columns. I crept past the mahogany clock in the entrance hall and the double front parlors with priceless Persian rugs. I made my way to the curved marble stairway. Mercedes was in a clothes closet, so that meant the second floor.

"Hello," Emmilene's voice echoed through the hall. "Harper Fowlkes House. Hello? Hello? Baby, is that you playing tricks to see if I'm still here? Well, I'm on my way, so pop the champagne and get out the caviar. We have those last few details to take care of, then we're home free."

I had no idea what Baby did, but it sure put Emmilene in a good mood. Emmilene went from boohoo for brother Corny to champagne and caviar in nine hours flat, setting some new speed record for family bereavement.

The stairway curved up around the brass chandelier, the master bedroom straight ahead. I could hear Emmilene scurrying about below to close things up. The lights clicked off one by one. The front door closed with a solid thud, casting the house in darkness. I sat on the steps and fished around in Old Yeller for my flashlight, something I kept on hand since stumbling across more than my share of dead bodies. The clock in the hallway below ticking away the minutes mixed with the creaks and groans of and old house settling in for the night. "Mercedes?"

I took the second doorway, my flashlight picking out the exquisite canopy bed, damask drapes, and cherry dressing table. Banging came from the back of the room. I jumped, turned and tripped over a humpback trunk.

"Reagan, that better be you out there making a bunch of racket, or I'm having a heart attack right this minute!"

I stumbled over to the closet and tried the handle. "There's no key in the lock."

"Say what!"

"Emmilene wouldn't take the key with her, so it's got to be

here somewhere. She's not the only one who gives tours. Let me check the dressing table."

"Check fast. I'm running out of air in here."

"The house was built in 1842 and leaks air like a sieve. You're fine."

"Not being locked in a closet is fine. And Reagan," Mercedes added in a hushed voice, "I smell cigar smoke."

Something creaked on the far side of the room. I whipped my flashlight in that direction then back and spied the key right there in the closet door lock. It was not there before. Was it?

"Found it."

"What's going on out there? Reagan! You sound strange. Are you okay?"

"Everything's fine." I opened the door, and Mercedes jumped out landing in my arms. "That front door better not be padlocked 'cause I'm barreling on through it like Wonder Woman on steroids. I've had enough of this place." Mercedes took my hand and yanked toward the hall, but I held back.

"The first-floor doors have alarms," I said. "Same with the first- and second-floor windows. There's a fire escape on the third floor, where they store stuff. There are only motion detectors on the first floor. They took out the ones on the second floor because of too many false alerts where no one was...was..."

Mercedes snagged the flashlight and held it up, her face lost in the darkness except for her two terrified brown eyes staring at me. "The police would come around, and no one was here?"

"Probably a bird or mouse got in."

"Or somebody never got out. Sweet baby Jesus in Heaven, how do I ever let you talk me into things like this?"

I took back the flashlight, snagged Mercedes' arm, and propelled her toward the doorway. The hallway narrowed, then narrowed again as we headed deeper into the house, our footfalls echoing against the wood floors.

"I smell cigars again."

"You smell old carpet, candle wax and lemon oil furniture polish." *And cigars.*

The steps creaked as we climbed up to the top floor with moonlight cutting a dull swathe across the old pine planks. A whiff of smoke swirled into the darkness.

"We go out there," I said to Mercedes, dragging her attention to the windows and away from the whiffing. "You have to unhook the bottom ladder of the fire escape and let it drop all the way down to the ground. It's that way to make it harder for anyone to climb up."

"You're sounding all weird again."

"It's been a long, weird day."

We cut around a claw-foot cherry table, Windsor chairs, and paintings with gilded frames. I unlatched the window and heaved it open, a cool, welcome breeze flowing in and clearing my head. City lights glimmered out across the city, and the garden fountain gurgled below.

"Guess this is a bad time to tell you that I'm not much fond of heights."

Something moved behind us, and Mercedes's eyes rounded to the size of golf balls. In a flash she had one foot out the window, followed by the other, and was halfway down the fire escape, her figure fading into the darkness. I climbed out onto the metal platform and turned to close the window. A red dot glowed in the far corner of the room-- brighter then fading then brighter again. The aroma of expensive cigars swirled around me.

"Thanks for the key," I whispered into the dark. I gently closed the window and headed down to the real world.

I POURED OUT A BOWL OF LUCKY CHARMS FOR ME, GOT BOONE'S

bowl of raisin oatmeal from the microwave, and scooped BW's morning kibble adding a generous dollop of pumpkin.

"Who's calling you so early?" I asked Boone. He came into our adorable kitchen with new white cabinets, fancy-dancy French-door refrigerator, and granite countertops that I loved and that would soon belong to Hollis.

"That was Aldeen."

"Good news?"

"Cops don't call with good news." Boone sat down at our table-for-two by the window that overlooked Auntie KiKi's backyard, bursting with purple and maroon mums. Boone added milk to the oatmeal then passed me the container. "She wanted to give me a heads up. Guess whose fingerprints they found on the Jen's and Friends napkin Corny had in his pocket?"

"Forensics keeps getting better and better." I spooned up the Lucky Charms, trying for the unicorn marshmallows. "That makes for more evidence against Auntie KiKi, as if finding Corny in her house wrapped in her hall rug wasn't enough. How are you going to get her out on bail now? Temporary insanity?"

Boone took a bite of oatmeal. "I'm playing the low-flight-risk card," he said around another mouthful. "She and Putter are married over forty years, and she's not about to leave him or the house that caused all this mess in the first place."

"Think it'll work?"

"Not a chance. But if she finds out someone's trying to usurp her presidency at the Garden Club, she'll tunnel out on her own."

Boone finished the last bite, snagged his jacket that he only wore for court, grabbed a to-go mug of coffee then kissed me dizzy. He stopped and looked deep into my eyes. "I know giving up this house is really hard, Reagan, and I hate like hell that I can't figure a way around it. If it's any consolation, you can decorate our new digs anyway you like."

"Floral chintz?"

Boone kissed me on the forehead then added a lopsided grin. "Even floral chintz."

Boone headed off to save Auntie KiKi, and I pushed colored marshmallows around my bowl, watching the milk swirl pink, purple, blue, and green. Even Lucky Charms didn't hold their usual appeal.

Last night, between bites of sandwich, I gave Boone the Cliffs Notes version of Emmilene, Mercedes and the Garden Club, to keep him in the loop. The part about the fire escape, not so much. Here's the thing with Boone. He was an attorney, meaning his duty was to uphold the law. He took the law seriously, and if he knew I did something illegal, that put him between a rock and Reagan. To avoid such predicaments, I felt it was my duty as wife to simply omit minor details.

But in my defense, since bad guys don't leave incriminating evidence out there in the open air for all to see, sometimes I-- along with Auntie KiKi and like-minded friends--got a little creative to find the truth. It's like Cher says, '*If you can't go straight ahead, you go around the corner.*' I did my share of cornering.

I put the breakfast bowls in the dishwasher—my new best friend-- and BW and I headed downstairs to open up the Fox. Sounds of hustle-and-bustle business floated our way, and it wasn't even ten. The shop was already hopping with Elsie and Annie Fritz in matching blue Prissy Fox aprons manning the counter. I'd left them in charge for two weeks while Boone and I honeymooned, so they had the keys. That they embroidered aprons was adorable.

"Time's a-wastin'." Annie Fritz tossed me a receipt pad then wrote up a sale for a denim jacket. BW scrambled behind the counter to get out of the way and catch a morning nap, and I hunted for a pen.

"Sister and I were having a nice pot of herbal tea with a splash of honey bourbon and chatting about what songs we need to be practicing for Cornelius McBride's funeral," Annie Fritz explained. "He wasn't the most adored individual on the plant so we're needing to pull out all stops. Then we happened to look out the window, and lo and behold, that Sleepy Pines van pulled up, and folks piled out. We figured you and Walker would be sleeping in and doing a little coochy-cooing, if you know what I mean. But since you're here now, I suppose not." Annie Fritz pulled a frown. "Love is done wasted on the young, if you ask me."

Elsie and Annie Fritz performed for weddings, but they were legendary as professional mourners. No one got folks a-weepin' and a-wailin' at a funeral like the Abbott sisters.

"And where is Mr. Hunky?" Zadie called from over by the blouse rack. Today Zadie was in pink jeans, pink blouse, and pink hat. "I sure could do with some nice eye-candy this morning to get my juices flowing. Fact is, we got enough money from our investment to bring him along on our Vegas trip to get my juices flowing every morning." Zadie twitched her well-rounded hips. "Once he gets a look at me in short-shorts with sequins on my butt, he'll be packing his bags and heading for the airport."

Zadie in sequins burned a frightening image into my brain, but what the heck, what happened in Vegas stayed in Vegas. Elsie led Zadie to the back window to hunt all things sequin, and Annie Fritz took in an armload of clothes to consider for consignment. Enos strolled up to the counter with a blue flowered shirt and straw hat in his hand.

"Sounds like you all have a great vacation planned." I wrote up the sale. "Did Zadie pick some really good investments? What stock was it? Amazon, Apple, Tesla?"

Enos handed over his credit card. "She estimated a timely

return on outlay, figured risk management, decided there was a definite dividend for everyone when it paid off, then we voted and made our decision. And it even paid off faster than we estimated."

"Tesla?"

"We took up with Cornelius McBride, and this time *we* came out on top."

Smiling ear to ear, Enos stuffed the shirt in his own cloth bag to avoid adding more plastic crap to the earth. "Time for tea and cookies," he called out. "Everybody get a move on. Today is chocolate chip day, and I got some tasty apricot brandy stashed away."

Enos led the Piners out the door, the little parade shuffling to the white van with *Sleepy Pines* scripted across the side parked at the curb. Hollis edged his way through the group, looking like a salmon going upstream. He stumbled to the checkout desk and dropped a big box in front of me. "Where should I put this?"

"Put what?" I said, trying to get my head around the Corny/Piners investment strategy.

"I'm moving in here, remember? This place is mine."

"Not for two weeks."

"If I bring in a few boxes here and there, I won't have to pay the money-grubbing movers as much." He glanced around. "Lou Ella's going to knock down this wall and go with one of those open-concept floor plans."

Hollis pointed to the dining room with racks of clothes all neatly arranged by size and color. Shelves of shoes and purses sat to the left, jackets and blazers to the right, men's apparel in the corner, and dresses to the back. Our old dining room table sat in the center, displaying jewelry and scarves and purses. A few years ago, the very same table displayed Hollis and Cupcake playing hide the salami. That I'd walked in on them gave a whole new meaning to 'table for two.'

"Lou Ella's event planner business will be a big hit here," Hollis babbled on. "And I already made the first payment on my new boat. I'm naming her Money Honey 'cause that's what I had the good sense to marry: a real live money-honey. I'll start a stack of boxes by the back door. Don't touch anything."

Elsie and Annie Fritz stared at me wide-eyed, and Hollis headed for the once-upon-a-time kitchen area done up in vintage wallpaper. Now it held the consigned furniture and Hollis's boxes.

"You're selling Cherry House?" Annie Fritz gasped.

"You and Walker just fixed the place up," Elsie added. "You got two bathrooms and granite countertops and us next door. What will we ever do?"

My heart cracked a bit. Cherry House was a possession. I should not get attached to possessions, but Cherry House, BW and I were a united rescue operation. I truly felt as if I were abandoning a friend. I studied the sad looks on Elsie and Annie Fritz's faces. Make that lots of friends.

"It's part of an agreement Hollis and I had that I sort of forgot about," I lied. "If I ever remarried, he'd get the house. Boone and I will move into his house, and I'm looking for a new space for the Prissy Fox. It's a new adventure. I'll come visit." I forced a smile.

"Well, that is absolutely the worst agreement I've ever heard in my whole entire life," Mamma said from the doorway with everyone in the shop nodding. "How come this is the first I've heard of you giving up Cherry House?"

I met Mamma at the door and led her out onto the front porch. We sat down on the top step with the morning sun creeping across the lawn and flowerbeds that needed weeding. "It's complicated."

"Honey, complicated is making Julia Child's beef bourguignon. This here is crazy talk. You've loved Cherry House since you were a kid visiting KiKi. You bought the place with money inherited from Nana Summerside. You did all the repairs because Hollis doesn't know a screwdriver from an army tank. He's always wanted this house, and now you're just handing it over."

Mamma stilled, her eyes widening. She bit her bottom lip. "Merciful heavens, you swapped."

I heaved a resigned sigh. "I told Hollis that the Rosegate deed would be tied up in courts forever, and he'd look like a total jerk and be a social outcast if he kicked Auntie KiKi and Uncle Putter out of their family home. KiKi knows that Hollis gave up his claim on Rosegate, but she doesn't know why. I'll give her the divorce story, but she'll figure it out like you did."

"No going back?"

"The agreement's signed and dated. Well, actually it's scrawled on the back of a Cakery Bakery receipt, but even with sprinkle smudges, it's still binding." Mamma gave me a hug, and I wiped away a tear. "How would you like to come with me to Sleepy Pines?"

"Your new address?"

That brought a smile. "The Piners teamed up with Corny for some kind of business venture. Now Corny's getting fitted for a casket, the investment paid off big-time, and the golden oldies are headed to Vegas on the profits. Corny swindled the Piners. At first, I didn't think that was enough for them to knock him off, but now with this business venture and him not being around to collect the profits..."

A sly grin spread across Mamma's lips. "Corny doesn't deserve to be six feet under, but the Piners now have their money back, and they got revenge. Corny thought they were an easy mark, and he could take advantage again. Then they turned the tables. Never underestimate a bunch of Southern seniors with a touch of Don Corleone swirling in their bones."

Mamma stood and pulled me beside her. "The only way to see if we're on the right track is to play it cool and follow the money."

"Especially when that money leads to Bonaventure Cemetery and Vegas."

CHAPTER 7

Mamma zoomed down Lincoln, hung a right onto Gaston, then onto Tatternal. She raced past the picket fence and squealed into the Sleepy Pines parking lot next to a police cruiser with its lights flashing. She killed the engine and swept back her hair. "This place sure is hopping."

"Mamma, did you ever think maybe you should drive a little slower so maybe you...don't get so stressed?" *And so I don't get so stressed,* I added to myself.

Mamma got out of the car and started for the patio. "Honey, your mamma thrives on stress. Besides, I haven't had a ticket in years."

I was pretty sure that was because no traffic cop wanted to risk life and limb in pursuit. I followed Mamma to the umbrellas and Piners enjoying midmorning coffee.

"Why, hi there, Reagan. Long time no see." Enos flashed a smile. "I sure hope you didn't ruin the suspension on that there nice black Caddy when you jumped the curb like you did."

I started to say that Mamma was at the wheel, but after my adventure of golf cart a-go-go yesterday, no one would believe it.

"Looks like you got a bit of trouble this morning?" I nodded at the police cruisers pulling away. "Is everyone okay?"

"Beatrice Bender and Amy Florbush are saying they had paintings they bought from me last year stolen right out of their rooms last night. But if you ask me, I think they went and gave those painting to some family member and forgot they did it. Happens all the time around here."

"Yep," Zadie chimed in. "Lots of forgetting going on, like where's my glasses? Where's my keys? Where's that cute little number I slept with last night?"

Not wanting a follow-up on the cute-number topic, I went with, "I'm here to thank you all for your business this morning." I held up a stack of flyers. "This gives you twenty percent off in case you forgot something."

"Well, how about that. I could use another sequin T-shirt to add a bit of zip and zing to the girls here." Zadie jutted her chest, befitting a twenty-something and underscoring the absolute marvels of modern-day nips and tucks. "Now that you're here, grab a cup and sit a spell. Your mamma can give us some tips on being lucky. The Silver Fox was a fancy-free widower for going on five years now, and none of us ever thought he'd settle down. Though I must say, some of us here did our best flirting when he came over to help with wills and such."

Mamma poured out the tea and handed me a cup. "You all have plenty of luck of your own. You're the ones heading off to Vegas for a week." Mamma took a sip and stared at her saucer. "It's a shame Corny's not around to enjoy the profits. I heard you all did some fine investing together."

"Together?" Enos laughed. "Well now, I suppose that is one way of looking at it. Corny was part of the investment deal for sure, but we never planned on him sharing in the payoff. That's not exactly how Don't Worry Die Happy works."

Mildred held up her teacup. "Don't Worry Die Happy."

Everyone did the same and echoed, "Don't Worry Die Happy."

JerryLee banged his cup on the table. "Okay, that's it. This foolishness has gone too far. I'll not have you talking about my nephew that way." Jerry Lee snagged his walker and thump-stepped his way through the double patio doors, slamming them shut behind him.

"We didn't mean to upset anyone by bringing up Corny," I said. "Maybe I should go apologize."

Mildred shook her head. "All that indignation is for show. JerryLee knows Corny hoodwinked him just like he did the rest of us, and deep down he feels mighty bad about it. Corny was always looking for a way to make a fast buck or con people any way he could. We didn't realize he did it to all of us until we got talking. Corny even double-crossed his own kin out of a family inheritance. We suspected that one day his double-dealing would come home to roost, and we decided to make that a payday for us."

Zadie held up her teacup and called out, "Don't Worry Die Happy."

"Don't Worry Die Happy!" Everyone saluted.

I said to Zelda, "Let me get this straight. You all took out a life insurance policy on Corny?"

"Yep. Everyone at the Pines wanted in, and JerryLee signed off on it. We needed his signature 'cause he's family. Only family can take out life insurance on another family member. The jury's still out if he really understood what was going on, but in the end, he's going to Vegas with the rest of us. Anyway, Irene said as long as we didn't get nailed for doing Corny in, we're home free, or in this case Vegas free. We do feel mighty bad KiKi wound up in jail over it."

I started to say that KiKi was innocent until a fifty-something lady in a flowered skirt, red blouse, and blond-streaked hair bounded into the room. "I do hate to break up a good party, but I got the van gassed up and waiting for you all back in the lot. If we're going to make Tybee for lunch, we got to hit the road now. We don't want Bubba Gumbo's running out of hushpuppies and honey butter on our watch now, do we?"

"Hushpuppies wait for no one." Mildred pushed herself up, with the rest of the Piners doing the same.

The van driver took hold of Jeb Wilcox's wheelchair and propelled it toward the gate until she spied Mamma at the table. She stopped dead, glaing at Mamma as if she were something nasty on the sidewalk. Then she jutted her chin and continued pushing the wheelchair.

"What was that all about?" I asked Mamma. "Did you lock up one of her relatives? Impound her car? Don't tell me you wore the same dress she did at the Telfair Christmas gala?"

Mamma and I headed for the Caddy in the back lot. "That's Irene Fairbanks. She used to be a nurse at St. Joseph's Hospital and had big eyes for Putter until KiKi and the shotgun convinced her that she didn't. But doesn't this all seem a little off?"

"That there's obviously bed-hopping going on, and Zadie has amazing implants?"

"I was thinking more about Irene being here with the Piners. They both just got what they wanted, and I'm not talking about lunch at Bubba Gumbo's."

We got in the car, and I stared at Mamma. "You think Irene and the Piners are in cahoots?"

"The polite term would be 'mutually beneficial alliance,' but 'in cahoots' works. The Piners knock off Corny for the money. Irene goes along to frame KiKi so she can get her hands on Putter...literally. Last year, Irene posted Putter's picture on Instagram with 'Don't be moody come shake my booty.' She showed up at the golf course over at Sweetmarsh Country Club too many times to count, and she even resorted to her car breaking down in front of Rosegate. That's when your dear aunt and the shotgun appeared on the scene."

I squelched a groan when Mamma backed over a once-lovely pink rosebush. "Except Uncle Putter thinks Instagram is a fast telegram, that anyone not playing golf is the caddy, and fixing a car means calling AAA. Uncle Putter's oblivious to all things except x-rays, golf, and pot roast, and he would never cheat on Auntie KiKi."

"Maybe, but it's all too convenient to be a simple coincidence, and a woman in love does some pretty crazy things."

Mamma shot down Liberty. I gritted my teeth and looked the other way to keep from screaming, and spotted Emmilene coming out of Mary Elizabeth's Exclusive Bridal Boutique. She carried a big white garment bag, and--having just bought the largest wedding dress in all Savannah myself--I knew that wedding dresses came in that size garment bag.

"Look," I yelped to Mamma. "Don't look!" *What was I thinking!* "I just saw Corny's sister coming out of Mary Elizabeth's with a wedding dress."

"Well, isn't that sweet as pie. At least she's getting on with her life, and we can wish her well. Maybe we should have a shower for her, considering the unfortunate circumstances in her life lately."

"Emmilene's scraping by to make ends meet. You and I both know that scraping by can't afford Mary Elizabeth, and now Emmilene can?"

"Kin!" Mamma pulled to an actual full stop at the traffic light...Lord be praised...and turned to me. "The kin Corny cut out of the family inheritance is his own sister? But you just don't buy a wedding dress off the rack from Mary Elizabeth. It has to be ordered months ago with half the money down. And then, the dress came in, and she had to pay the balance. Seems pretty convenient that Corny's dead when Emmilene needs a quick infusion of cash. But would someone really kill for a wedding dress?"

I rolled my eyes. "Mamma, you've seen *Say Yes to the Dress.* You went wedding-dress shopping with me. Look at the dress I bought. Brides and their wedding dresses are not to be parted. If she planned a big reception and honeymoon, the bills are coming in."

Mamma hit the gas, and we blasted off. "The who-done-it list for knocking off Corny keeps on growing. We got the Piners, Irene, and now Emmilene. There'll be a ton of people at that man's funeral when they finally release the body. In spite of the Abbott sisters' heartfelt warbling, I imagine the guests won't be shedding many tears."

Mamma dropped me off in front of the Fox, and I resisted the urge to kiss the pavement. Instead, I waved as Mamma headed off to the Old Pink House for lunch of shrimp and grits while I anticipated sharing a veggie hotdog with BW. I was truly happy for Mamma and her new love-life and also a bit envious of the shrimp and grits.

"You're back already," I said to Boone, who stood behind the counter, writing up a sale for a blue straw hat. "How'd it go?"

"Annie Fritz and Elsie needed to practice dead songs for Corny's funeral, so I'm pinch-hitting." Boone was a true Renaissance Man: lawyer in the morning; delish retail clerk in the afternoon; sexy lover at night.

"And your favorite auntie is home, sort of." Boone handed the dreamy-eyed customer her bag and added a smile guaranteed to bring her back for more shopping. That sales doubled whenever Boone manned the counter didn't surprise me one bit.

"You got her out of jail?" I hopped behind the counter and planted a kiss on Boone's cheek. "You're amazing."

"Hold that thought. There's a catch." Boone wrote up a sale

for a taupe dress and strappy heels. That I was also at the counter and could write the sale probably did not enter the smitten customer's mind.

"When I say KiKi's home," Boone said when we were alone, "I mean she has to stay there, or at least not go any farther than the end of the property line."

"Dog collar?"

"House arrest and ankle monitors. It was KiKi's idea, though she did make a fuss that the monitors didn't come in an assortment of designer colors. She insisted that Putter's health depended on her cooking and caring for him."

"Let me guess: the judge had Uncle Putter do his bypass?" I took in a skirt, sweater, and a pair of leather ankle booties to consign. Boone sat down on the little stool and scratched BW behind the ears.

"The judge's wife had the bypass. The thing is, I know KiKi. We all know KiKi, and there is no way she's staying put in her house. Somehow, someway, she'll be out hunting the killer, and house arrest be damned. I'm responsible for her."

"She can't go far." I hung up the skirt and sweater. "How much trouble can she get into in her own house?"

"Why does that not reassure me? KiKi said she had personal business to tend to and she'd call you later." Boone stood and wrapped his arm around me, drawing me close. A hint of his woodsy aftershave drifted my way, making me a little light-headed, very turned on, and wanting to jump his bones right there in the hallway.

"Whatever KiKi's got cooking up, and we know there's something," Boone said, "try not to get me in too much trouble, okay? Your mom's a judge, and now she's dating a judge. With a little bad luck, I could spend our first anniversary in an orange jumpsuit." Boone looked down at me. "Hey, are you okay?"

"No."

"Sweething, we really need a honeymoon." Boone heaved a resigned sigh, gave me a sloppy kiss, then headed off to meet with Big Joey. If anyone knew about the shady side of Corny, it was Big Joey and the Seventeenth Street Gang.

I wrote up a sale for an ugly green blouse and took in a small rose arbor plus a metal garden statue of a crane with a fish in its mouth. I assigned a number for the new account and had the customer okay the official Prissy Fox agreement form as a young guy with blond, stringy hair swaggered in the door. He dropped a really nice leather jacket on the counter.

"I wanna sell this, and don't try and con me like you do everybody else. I know what a Burberry jacket goes for."

"This is a consignment shop. We don't buy clothes outright. You leave the jacket, and after it sells, we split the profits fifty-fifty."

"It's my jacket. I should get seventy-five percent."

"Like Cher says, 'Somebody's got to pay for the frogs and dancing fairies.'"

"What the heck's that supposed to mean?" He shook his head. "Never mind. Make me an offer."

How about I offer to kick your pompous butt out the door? was on the tip of my tongue, but this was a business opportunity. I didn't want to lose the jacket sale. I flipped open the lid of my Godiva candy box that served as my cash register. Yeah, yeah, yeah. I should upgrade, but truth be told, I loved the smell of chocolate every time I made a sale. It was like a little reward for owning my own shop. I pulled out some bills and counted them out. "I'll buy it outright because I know I can sell it, but this is the best I can do."

Blondie swooped up the bills and jammed them in his jeans pocket. "Better than nothing. Being poor sucks." He stormed off, and I held up the jacket, size large. It didn't belong to Blondie, size medium. It was in style, wouldn't be around the shop long, and I wished I could say the same for Hollis stumbling up my sidewalk yet again. I stifled a groan as he waddled to the counter and dropped down two more boxes.

"These are really heavy."

"You could just wait for the movers. That is why they're called 'movers.'"

"Ya know, this place is really starting to feel like home. It never did before when I lived here. Then it was rundown and ugly. But now, it's kind of okay." A sly grin spread across Hollis's face. He leaned on one of the boxes, crushed in the corner, and added a confident shrug. "It's been quite a day for me. Some people, well, actually quite a few people, are calling me a hero for not throwing the Vanderpools out of their house. I even got an invite to join the Savannah Yacht Club."

Hollis's chest puffed out two inches. "The word spread pretty quick about me doing the right thing about Rosegate. But that's what's expected of a Beaumont. The family is a pillar of the Savannah community. In fact, Mother did one of those *23andMe* DNA research tests showing how we're related to the oldest and finest families in Savannah. Lou Ella really loved that. She's having the family tree framed. That Scarlett Rose person from *People Want to Know* is going to interview me on her show about the Savannah families who've given so much."

"Key to the city forthcoming?"

"I'm working on it. Oh, and by the way, Davis is coming this afternoon to measure for an antique bookshelf that Lou Ella has her eye on. I figure I can splurge on furnishings to keep my little workhorse happy."

The hero story I expected since Hollis leaked it; the proud family reference I'd heard ad nauseam and was no doubt tattooed on his butt; the workhorse crack was typical Hollis.

"Davis who?"

"What am I, Google? Some guy with a bookshelf. If that

Scarlett Rose person comes knocking, say nice things. Remember I'm doing you a favor, and you owe me big time."

Hollis strolled off, and for the rest of the day I was up to my eyeballs in clothes and sales. That was a good thing since come January, the Fox was deader than Lincoln, or more recently Corny McGuire.

I closed at six and fed BW his dinner in the shop so he wouldn't be eating alone. I needed to straighten up the mess left by shoppers and ready the place for tomorrow. I had so few tomorrows left, and I really needed to look for a new Prissy Fox and start packing up our home. That thought was enough to depress a hyena.

I got a text from Boone that he and Big Joey would meet me at Jen's and Friends at eight, and from the kitchen area came, "Yoo-hoo, honey. I'm home."

"KiKi? KiKi! What the heck are you doing here?" I said as she strolled down the hallway.

"Why, I do believe that's the very thing the South said to the North when they crossed the Ohio River."

I ran over to Auntie KiKi, grabbed her hand and tried to drag her back to the kitchen and shoo her out the rear door. "You have to stay home and that means *your* home. When you leave, some alarm thing goes off somewhere and the cops come running. There'll be lots of sirens, and you'll be right back in jail. How did you get so strong?" I gave KiKi another tug. "You're not budging an inch."

"It's my three-olive-martini regimen." Auntie KiKi fluffed her hair. "Extra vegetables build muscle and..." KiKi held out her ankle. "And what little ol' anklet are you talking about, honey?"

"You can't just cut the thing off! It's not a hospital bracelet. You don't just get rid of it when you walk out the door. The monitor has sensors and a GPS tracking gadget. Uncle Putter will have a full-blown conniption when he finds you gone."

"I convinced the dear man to attend that symposium in Atlanta. I told him you had a list of suspects lined up, and were close to finding the killer, and I was safe at home with my anklet."

"You told him what!"

"And can I help that the ugly thing magically slipped off my ankle all by itself," Auntie KiKi added ignoring my protest. "Okay, I might have used some extra virgin olive oil to facilitate the slipping, though I have no idea what this 'extra virgin' is all about. I mean, either you are or aren't and--"

"KiKi, what have you done!"

She cleared her throat. "It was all a matter of diet. The guards over at the police station are the worst poker players on the planet. Instead of paying me off, I had them bring in ham and salami, potato chips, and those spicy nuts in the little blue can. You saw the biscuits and gravy. Then I got Max's fried chicken extra-crispy, delivered to make sure."

"Of what? That you'd set a speed record for gaining ten pounds and sending your cholesterol through the roof?"

"That I'd swell up like a balloon from a big old sodium over-dose. That bossy old policewoman with the mustache...can we say tweezers?...fitted me with the anklet this morning. I was so bloated I couldn't even get my shoes on. I kept complaining that the anklet was too tight, and she had to loosen it up three times. When I got home, all I had to do was--"

"You drank a ton of water and took diuretic pills."

"Then peed like a racehorse for the next five hours, but now I'm good to go. Well, *not go*, at least for a while."

I pinched the bridge of my nose and tried not to pop blood vessels. "That is a totally unhealthy thing to do."

"Rotting in jail for a murder I didn't commit is not a trip to the Four Seasons Spa, dear. I tied the anklet around Princess then scattered catnip all over the house, so it looks like I'm walking about. I saw a TV show once where this adorable man put his anklet on the dog. It worked for him, though he didn't use the virgin olive oil. Actually, I'd say there wasn't one thing virgin about that sexy hunk. And since we don't hear those sirens, I think we're in the clear. Now, I need some clothes."

"You have more clothes than Macy's."

Auntie KiKi wandered into the dining room/show room. "I'm thinking thirty-four short."

"Short's a given, and you can shave off a few years, but thirty-four might be a bridge too far."

KiKi held up a pinstripe men's suit. "I can't go out looking like KiKi Vanderpool, and we've used the old-lady disguise before. We gotta mix things up tonight."

"We? Tonight?"

"Jen's and Friends was where this whole thing went off the rails, so that's the logical place to start. I need to find that waiter. The one who delivered my note. Corny was bragging on and on about his ship coming in, and maybe the waiter remembers someone following Corny out of the bar. Someone knew that I was meeting Corny at Rosegate. If they saw me in the park, they could have hatched the plan to frame me."

"Do you remember the waiter's name?"

"After three martinis, I'm lucky to remember my own name. Young man, I think. Youngish. And he had an apron, or was it a vest? And pants, or maybe shorts. And a shirt. Did he have a ponytail? Not sure about the shirt." Auntie KiKi pulled a gray fedora from the rack over the suits, slid it on, stuffed her red hair under and added a scowl. "This is perfect. Now I look like Sean Connery."

CHAPTER 8

"We'll park the Beemer in the lot behind Jimmy John's and cut through to Jen's and Friends," Auntie KiKi said to me when we passed Johnson Square and made a right onto West Congress. Johnson Square was the largest and oldest of the twenty-three with two fountains, and a monument to William Bull, who helped lay out the city, and where they read aloud to everyone the Declaration of Independence back in 1776. How cool is that!

"People recognize my Foxtrot license plate, so parking on the street is too risky," Auntie KiKi added. "I'm not taking any chances of getting sent back to jail with Officer Mustache."

I looked at Auntie KiKi in her pinstripe and fedora. "Uncle Putter wouldn't recognize you in this getup."

"He would if I had a dish of pot roast in my hand." Auntie KiKi pulled into the lot and killed the engine. "I used a Sharpie to give myself a little scruff." KiKi jutted her chin in my direction. "What do you think?"

"You have waxed eyebrows, pierced ears and a fifty-dollar manicure. You as a guy is a tough sell."

"Yeah, but I can drink with the best of 'em."

We climbed out of the Beemer, and Auntie KiKi clicked the lock button. Streetlight spilled into the lot, and we cut around the other cars to a scraggly row of bushes separating the lot from the back of Jimmy John's. We wiggled through some dead branches to a dented green dumpster and a stack of cardboard boxes tied up for recycle.

"If something slithers out, I'm screaming my head off, just so you know."

We took the corner and started down the narrow alley with the back wall of Jen's and Friends up ahead. Wood pallets leaned against the concrete-block building, and two men stood under a light swarming with insects.

"I think I saw a rat." Auntie Kiki drew up close, her breath on my neck.

"It was probably a cat." *It was probably a rat.* I took KiKi's hand, and we walked faster. "Almost there."

The men's voices rose, with the taller, older guy shaking his finger at the shorter blond one. "You're thirty next week. Are you ever going to get your act together?"

"I know that guy," I whispered to KiKi. "I know both of them."

"Did you just step on my foot? I think there's more than two of us in here."

"Is that why you called me?" the shorter guy said. "More lectures? I got a job, I got friends, and you're not my father, so buzz off."

"You flunked out of college, flunked out of the police academy, and now you have Pixie Stix straws sticking out of your pocket. What's next, Simon? Pink bunny ears and a fluffy tail on your butt?" The man waved a handful of papers. "You're overdrawn at the bank and racking up loans. They repossessed your car that I co-signed for. You're killing my credit score."

"Next month I'm getting that big raise, remember. This isn't your courtroom, and I don't have to hang around and listen to you."

I whispered to KiKi, "That's Judge Swain, and that kid brought in a leather jacket to the Fox."

"I don't care if it's Darth Vader and he brought in his Batmobile," KiKi whispered back, doing a little fidget dance. "I want the blazes out of this here alley."

"He's Mamma's main squeeze. We need to scope him out. And Darth Vader does not have a Batmobile and shush."

Shush got me the look of death. The young guy turned and left, and something darted between my legs and swished past Auntie KiKi.

"Holy saints above, it's wild America!" KiKi ran into the clearing, sprinted past Swain, and zipped into the backdoor of Jen's and Friends, the screened door banging shut behind her.

Swain looked from Auntie KiKi to me in the alley, his eyes widening in recognition. "Reagan?"

I stepped into the light and hitched my head toward the screened door. "A shy friend who really wanted a martini. Are you okay? It looked a little tense there."

The judge raked his hand through his usually perfect silver hair. "My son. Make that stepson."

Who just sold me your leather Burberry jacket.

"We don't get along," Swain added. "Virginia's passing just made things worse. She was the only thing we had in common other than Mario Kart and football. Simon was a decent quarterback till the University of Florida kicked him out." Swain gave me a weak grin. "So, how did your mamma raise the perfect daughter?"

"I married Hollis Beaumont, I'm on a permanent watch list with the Savannah police department, and there was a dead guy at my wedding." I added a shrug. "Not so perfect."

"You better catch up with your auntie, or she'll start drinking without you. I hear they're naming a martini in her honor, the Miss KiKi. It's served with a sugar rim, candy necklace, and a shot of vanilla vodka on the side."

"You know that was KiKi?"

"I had an auntie like that. Ever been to Lizzy's down on River Street? They named the whole bar after her. She took me there for my first drink when I turned sixteen." Swain laughed then sobered. "Good luck on finding the killer. KiKi didn't murder McBride. After years on the bench, I got a feel for these things. She's lucky to have you in her corner."

Shoulders bent, the judge shuffled toward the side street, gravel crunching under his feet as he faded into the shadows. I didn't know Swain all that well, but I could see why Mamma had a thing for him. I liked him. That he thought Auntie KiKi was innocent and that I was the perfect daughter might have had a little something to do with my decision.

Instead of cutting through the bar and interrupting staff yet again, I detoured around to the front of J&F, framed in white stucco arches. Bar chatter and tables with maroon umbrellas filled the sidewalk area, cordoned off for enjoying martinis alfresco. Auntie KiKi plus one, namely Big Joey, sat off to the side.

"He didn't even know who I was," Auntie KiKi gushed. I sat down, and Big Joey gave me an eyeroll. KiKi added, "I should be one of those undercover police people. I bet I'd catch a lot of bad guys."

"Right now, you be the bad guy." Big Joey's eyes twinkled over the rim of his glass, then he leaned back in his chair that looked about two sizes too small. Tonight, he wore his usual black jeans and black T-shirt, stretched across a fit six-pack and showing off well-toned biceps. He had a slight scruff, hair pulled back into a ponytail, and his complexion--along with choice of wardrobe and shadows--nearly made the man invisible. The operative word being *nearly.*

Everyone in Savannah knew Big Joey. Whereas gangs were not something to aspire to, the Seventeenth Street rescued more than one kid. They gave him a home, education, a job, and set him on the straight and narrow. My new husband was one of those kids.

"Didn't know this was your watering hole of choice," I said to Big Joey after I ordered a strawberry shortcake martini instead of the usual Snickers. "Thought you were more an Abe's on Lincoln kind of guy."

"True dat. Coke Zero be Coke Zero, and J&F keep it chill with a gummy bear." Big Joey popped the red bear in his mouth, his smile white against the dark except for the single gold tooth catching the light. "And your man had a meet with Ross, saying this be the place for Ms. KiKi's evening inquiry. In addition, yours truly has items of interest."

The waitress set down my drink that was more dessert than alcohol with skewered strawberry, chunk of cake, and dab of whipped cream. I finger-swiped the cream and licked it off. Big Joey leaned into the table, and Auntie KiKi and I did the same, figuring something important big was about to spill. See, I was getting pretty good at this street jive.

"The Corn," Big Joey said in a low, mellow voice, "did the dotted line on the Noah Knapp, and the street say a deuce back he dis old Gillespie to get the shop and wash the Benjamins."

"Corny bought the Noah Knapp House over on Jones Street?" I translated to make sure I got things straight. "And he somehow harassed Gillespie to be partners in I Do Declare? You lost me on washing Benjamins. I have no idea who they are and why they're dirty."

Big Joey looked pained and took a sip of Coke. "Creating a financial action establishment."

"Money laundering." KiKi flashed a smug grin and stroked her Sharpie scruff. "I drink. I know stuff. I binge *The Wire*."

Big Joey did another eyeroll, this one so far back in his head I thought he'd flip out of the chair. Auntie KiKi said, "You got to give the devil his due. An auction house could play loosey-goosy with how much he gets for a sale. That can make for some creative bookkeeping to hide Corny's ill-gotten gains if he's doing to others what he was doing to me. He couldn't exactly show up at the bank with a suitcase full of money to buy an expensive house on Jones Street without some questions being asked."

"But what could Corny have on Gillespie to let him be a partner?" I took a sip of martini that really did taste like strawberry shortcake with a kick. "IDD had a good name till Corny got his mitts into it."

Auntie KiKi bit the Snickers off the end of the skewer then held up her glass to get a refill. Her brows suddenly narrowed, and she lowered the martini glass. She drew in a sharp breath. "Uh-oh."

I shook my head at Auntie KiKi. "Forget *uh-oh*. We do not need *uh-oh*. Only rainbows and unicorns allowed, or we'll never get you out of jail."

"I'll have you know this *uh-oh* is all about doing the rainbow thing," KiKi huffed. "I went and bought that *Golf Is a Many Splendored Thing* painting from Gillespie for Putter's birthday, but the insurance man said the painting was a big old knockoff. I sure didn't pay a knockoff price. I told Gillespie and promised to keep it just between us, not wanting to ruin his reputation and all. I never had the heart to tell Putter the painting was a forgery. He was so excited when I had it delivered. That nice young man even hung it over the fireplace right above the shotgun. Putter's birthday is coming up, making two years ago that I bought the forgery." Auntie KiKi held up two fingers. "Two years. Deuce."

"You think Corny blackmailed Gillespie about the painting? But how did Corny find out about the forgery in the first place?"

"Heavenly days and Lord take me now." Auntie KiKi jabbed her skewer, with the last dab of Snickers attached, toward the doorway. "That's the boy I gave my note to for Corny."

Trying not to look obvious--though the *take me now* crack pretty much sank that ship--I cut my gaze to the doorway. "It's Swain's son. He was in the alley when we were there. Don't you remember?"

"All I recall about that alley is a rat doing his business on Putter's Italian loafers and scaring the bejeebers out of me. I need to talk to that waiter right quick before he gets away." Auntie KiKi jumped out of her chair, snatched her fedora midair, and slapped it back on her head.

Big Joey asked, "Are you two always like this?"

"Nah." I kissed Big Joey on the cheek. "You caught us on a slow night." I took a quick last gulp of shortcake, snagged Old Yeller, and followed KiKi. She wound her way through the maze of tables and patrons, Big Joey following me, our little parade homing in on Simon Swain.

"Remember me?" KiKi asked over the din as she drew up next to Simon. "I was here last Friday night. It was kinda late? Me paying you to pass on a napkin to Corny McBride?"

Simon scribbled on his order pad. "We were slammed with a martini party in the back room." He gave Auntie KiKi a quick look. "I got to say, you'd be a real tough one to forget. But I know her." Simon nodded at me. "I sold her my jacket."

"Forget the jacket," Auntie KiKi huffed. "I didn't look like this on Friday."

"I don't have time for this. There's a bunch of old farts partying in the back room, and I got to get drinks going and..."

Big Joey stepped into view, folded his arms across his chest, and Auntie KiKi continued with "Think of me with auburn hair and wearing a lovely purple dress and having the grace of a true Southern belle with a bit of sass. Corny McBride was that little guy at the end of the bar with a bad toupee, three pack a day complexion and running his mouth about landing the silver tuna." Auntie KiKi flashed a toothy grin. "Meet the silver tuna."

"Look, Corny was one bad dude. Had stuff on people and made 'em pay. No one's going to miss Corny McBride. He's dead, lady. Forget about him and go home."

"I can't forget him. I'm the one accused of making him dead. Do you remember anyone who followed Corny out of the bar when he left? Maybe someone who had it in for Corny?"

Simon's eyes widened. He took another step back and bumped into a waitress, nearly sending two cotton candy martinis to the floor. He lowered his voice. "You're supposed to be in jail. I can't be talking to an escaped convict. Have a martini on me. Have two. Have a Pixie Stix." Simon handed a blue straw to Auntie KiKi then stumbled off, fading into the crowd.

"You scared the life right out of that little dude," Big Joey said with a chuckle. He threaded his way to the exit with Auntie KiKi.

I took a detour. Maybe because I liked the judge, or because he was involved with Mamma, or maybe because I'd made my share of mistakes and thought I could possibly help. I snagged Simon's arm.

"Don't give your dad such a hard time. He's looking out for you. Maybe you could cut him some slack and meet him halfway. I saw you in the alley."

"He's not my dad, and the wonderful Judge Swain isn't the goody-goody you think he is. You need to mind your own freaking business and get out of mine."

Simon yanked his arm and walked away. I sidestepped my way through the customers, feeling like an idiot for getting involved, and met up with Auntie KiKi and Big Joey on the sidewalk.

"What happened to you?" KiKi wanted to know. "Not that it matters because Big Joey and I got some big decisions going on here. Mac and cheese bowl or a pulled pork sandwich?"

Auntie KiKi pointed across the street to Johnson Square and the Bowtie Barbecue food truck with the piggy in a red bowtie painted on the side. It was parked at the corner. "I never did get that second martini, so I'm thinking mac and cheese and pulled pork might be in order."

Big Joey rubbed the back of his neck then peered down his nose at Auntie KiKi. "How a little lady like you eat and drink me under the table?"

Auntie KiKi batted her eyes. "I drink like a sailor and say please and thank you like a saint. I'm a complicated woman."

Big Joey shuffled off for the truck while Auntie KiKi and I headed for the bench by the marble obelisk that honored Nathanael Greene. Of course, the square was named after South Carolina governor Johnson and not Greene because naming it after Greene would have made way too much sense.

"Some night," Big Joey said as he passed out the white Styrofoam containers of pure deliciousness. "Waste of time. The wacked waiter at J&F an epic fail."

"Fail?" Auntie KiKi's head snapped up, and her gaze fused with mine. I did the little head-shake thing and nodded at Big Joey, hoping Auntie KiKi would get the message to keep her mouth shut about what we did find out from Simon. Big Joey was Boone's brother in every way but parentage. The more Boone knew what Auntie KiKi and I were up to, the more he'd worry.

"Yep," I said, licking the cheese off my spork. "Pretty much a dead end there."

"Yep, not a single clue, nuh-uh." Auntie KiKi scooped up more gooey pasta. "Blind alley, end of the road, utterly useless, zero success, nada."

Subtleness was never KiKi's strong suit, so, thank heavens, her phone chirped before she rambled on even more about Simon. She pulled the phone from her suit pocket, made a face at the screen and pursed her lips. "It's Putter. I have to go home right this minute. I couldn't pick up his call here, with all the traffic noise, or he'd know I was out and about. If he tries the landline at the house and I don't pick up there, he might suspect I'm up to something, considering my present situation with the police."

"Might?" Big Joey arched both brows.

"Putter believes I'm the perfect Southern belle he married forty-five years ago. He thinks of me as his little lady who teaches ballroom dancing, stays home and bakes and watches Martha Stewart cooking shows."

"He doesn't know your rep...no disrespect...as a...wild woman?"

Auntie KiKi giggled and tipped her fedora. "Only in the bedroom, dear. Only in the bedroom." KiKi tossed her empty container in the garbage receptacle, then patted Big Joey's cheek, now blushing clear through its natural shade.

I closed my Styrofoam container, deciding to save the rest for Boone and BW and to spare my waistline. "It would be nice to salvage something of my honeymoon," I said. "I'm calling it a night too."

Auntie KiKi and I thanked Big Joey for food, drinks and info then headed for the crosswalk. We wedged ourselves between the parked cars then dodged a scooter put-putting around the cobblestone square. We jumped out of the way of a white van barreling toward us then sidestepped a tour trolley. In Savannah, getting to the other side of the road was more Olympic sport than God-given right. The chicken never would have made it.

"Is Big Joey still at the truck?" I asked Auntie KiKi when we turned into the parking lot. "I got this weird feeling we're being watched."

Auntie KiKi did a quick look back to the park. "He's chatting it up with the guy in the food truck like they're long-lost buddies. I thought for sure Big Joey would pick up on Simon mentioning that Corny had stuff on people he knew. Corny had money coming in, all right. Laundering money through the auction house means Corny kept two sets of books. One for the IRS and clients. One for Corny. Those books are how we find out who Corny had his claws into, and who would want him gone."

Auntie KiKi unlocked the Beemer. "We'll take the back entrance out of here and cut over to the auction house. With a little luck, the cops haven't scoured the place yet, and we'll have a crack at looking around for the second set of books. We know Corny swindled the Piners. With Gillespie being one of the gang at the Pines, that makes their motive stronger than ever. We need to find out who else that slimy varmint had on the hook."

"Wait, what! Gillespie lives at Sleepy Pines?"

"Enos Gillespie, dear. That poor man went and had a stroke a while back. We all assumed it was one of the reasons he took on Corny as a partner to help him out. Now it all makes sense. Corny was the reason Enos got that stroke in the first place. And why are you just standing here staring at me all wide-eyed and not getting yourself in the car? Make it snappy, we're on a mission. Freedom's in the air, I can smell it."

"That's the Kerry flavor plant doing up a batch of vanilla that you're smelling, and there is no way you're going with me to IDD. Remember Uncle Putter and your landline?"

Auntie KiKi opened the car door, tossed her fedora in the back seat and fluffed her hair. "Well, shut my mouth and hand me an Oscar. That was one of those horrid robo calls we all get. I figured we needed an excuse to make tracks for the auction house, and the fake call was it. Once Putter gets to those medical convention places, he's in the world of ICU, MRI, CBC, PCP, and all the rest of the medical alphabet soup. Until someone brings up golf, of course. Then it's to blazes with curing the world and on to the really important things of life, like hitting a little white ball into a hole."

"If you get caught breaking into IDD, it could be really bad."

Auntie KiKi flashed a grin and wrinkled her nose. "Getting caught isn't part of the plan."

"Foxtrot can't be anywhere near there."

"We'll throw mud on the license plate."

"You need to go home. And you need to hope Princess didn't chew through the anklet, and that policewoman Mustache isn't waiting with cruiser and blue lights flashing. I'll text you."

KiKi stuck out her bottom lip in a perfect auntie pout. "I'm hating this something fierce, you know."

"You hate being left out, but you'd hate making license plates and eating off a tin tray even more."

I watched Auntie KiKi drive out of the lot, then I peeked around the corner to make sure Big Joey wasn't lingering. I tucked the leftover mac and cheese container into Old Yeller, wishing I'd brought a sweater against the fall chill. I headed for Liberty. With a little luck, Boone would think I was with Big Joey and Big Joey would think I was headed home to Boone. But I couldn't count on that luck for long. I'd have to do a quick in and out at the auction house and hope to find evidence that incriminated someone other than Fedora Girl, aka Savannah's answer to Sean Connery.

CHAPTER 9

A harvest moon hung low on the horizon, bobbing in and out of view as I crossed Drayton. I passed Starbucks then Pelindaba Lavender. Starbucks was okay for a quick caffeine hit, but Pelindaba's linen closet cachets made the shop a true Savannah fave.

Up ahead sat a white clapboard house sporting a front door with yellow Do Not Cross tape and a wide veranda with battered wicker furniture. An I Do Declare sign needing a repaint, was suspended from the eaves and swayed gently in the night breeze. In another life, the house was a lovely home, but now the back rooms were for viewing auction and sale items. The living room and dining room were combined into one big space for bidders.

Businesses were closed for the night, foot traffic nonexistent, and cars focused on gunning it to the green light at the intersection. But this was Savannah, ground zero for busybodies and gossip. Me loitering at a dead guy's business wouldn't go unnoticed. No doubt the first floor had an alarm; the second floor, not so much. Hoisting a mahogany Chippendale dining room table up the stairs and out a window was a bit over the top even for the most avid Savannah antique thief. Jewelry and smaller collectables would be stashed in a safe.

Needing to get out of sight, I hustled down the narrow driveway between IDD and Gilbert's Art Supplies and came out into the weed-choked back yard. A lone light bulb dangled from a socket, casting shadows between trashcans. Discarded furniture was piled up in a bonfire-ready-for-match fashion. An overhang protected the back door from the elements and gave me a way in through the window above. If I could get onto the overhang and reach that window without breaking my neck.

I balanced a chair with no back on a table with a big hole in the middle. I scooted cabinets missing drawers over for support then held on to a rusted floor lamp for balance. I hoisted Old Yeller onto my shoulder and crawled up on to the table. It wobbled, the whole structure listing left, and I fast reached for the windowsill. I grabbed hold, steadied, slowly stood and--

"A girl could go to jail for doing that," came from below.

I jerked around, spied Boone and lost my footing, sending table, chair and cabinets flying. I held on to Old Yeller for dear life and fell butt first into Boone's arms. Anne Hathaway would have made it look good. I was not Ann Hathaway. "What are you doing here?"

Boone brushed back my hair, kissed me then and then set me down. "I think that's my line, and I wasn't kidding about jail."

"I got a good lawyer on speed-dial, and how'd you know I'd be poking around?"

"Husband telepathy." Boone took off his jacket and draped it around my shoulders.

"Meaning Big Joey ratted me out. I knew he was playing dumb. Look, you're a lawyer and upstanding man of the law, and you can't be any part of what I'm doing. In fact, you shouldn't even know what I'm doing."

"Story of my life."

"But since you are handsome," I added a kiss, "and gallant," I added another kiss, "and an innocent bystander, you can give me a leg up." I pointed at the window.

"No way am I letting you go in there."

"Here's the thing. Corny found out that Enos Gillespie sold Auntie KiKi a fake painting. He threatened to tell everyone and blackmailed Enos into being a partner in I Do Declare. That way Corny could launder money from his nefarious enterprises."

"The two-sets-of-books scenario. Big Joey told me about Corny buying a big house on Jones Street. That's prime Savannah real estate. Old Corny had the gooks on a lot of people."

"And he planned on adding Auntie KiKi." I dug my phone out of my purse and made Flippy do a little air dance. "You stay here and be the lookout, and we'll walkie-talkie. It'll be just like you're with me if I get into trouble." I put the back of my hand to my forehead and batted my eyes. "I can call 'Oh, Boone, my darling man, come save me' and,"--I pulled out the mac and cheese container from Old Yeller "in the meantime, you can eat."

Boone eyed the container, drool forming at the corner of this mouth. "You really think you can bribe me with food?"

"You're a guy who hasn't eaten in probably two hours, and I have sustenance from BowTie Barbecue. Slam dunk."

I righted the table, dropped my purse on top and stuck my phone and flashlight in the jacket pocket. I put one foot in Boone's cupped hands, the other on his shoulder. He put his hand on my behind for reasons that had nothing to do with leverage. I scrambled onto the little roof, hoping something didn't scramble onto me. "The window's locked. Who locks a second-story window?"

"Somebody with something to hide," Boone said around a mouthful. "Come on down before you get hurt."

I took off the jacket, wrapped it around my hand and smacked the end of the flashlight against the pane.

"What-the-hell-are-you-doing! I just bit off the end of the freaking spork!"

"Don't swallow." I gave Boone a cheeky thumbs-up then brushed away the shards with the jacket sleeve. Carefully, so as not to sever an artery, I reached inside and undid the latch. I pried open the window, laid the jacket carefully over the shattered glass to avoid more artery severing, hoisted my leg inside, lost my balance and toppled in head-first. I got out my phone and hit #1 on speed-dial. "Houston, the eagle has landed."

"The eagle crash-landed."

"Looks like Corny lived here. Got thoughts as to where he'd hide a ledger?"

"Behind the toilet."

I shivered and gagged. "Think something else."

"Freezer."

I clicked on the flashlight and scanned it across a room jammed with furniture. Really nice furniture. Hoarding for his new digs? An unmade, but really cool, brass bed crowded one side of the room next to a floor lamp decorated with a dirty shirt and pants. Stacks of leather-bound books were piled on two blue brocade wingback chairs. Rolled Oriental rugs leaned against the far wall, and my beam reflected off the brass pendulum of a grandfather clock befitting the Telfair Museum. "Corny's an elegant slob," I reported to Boone.

"A ruthless, elegant slob. He wouldn't have the ledger out of his sight. He'd be adding to it on a daily basis, so it's not in a safety deposit box somewhere. Think like a crook."

"Right now, I am a crook." I held my breath and felt under the mattress. If I came across porn, I'd have to sterilize my hands and replace my eyeballs. I opened the closet door and pushed back clothes slung over hangers. Hoping for a hollow spot where the ledger might be stored, I knocked on the back and sides of solid plaster walls. I checked the brocade chairs and looked through the books to make sure the ledger wasn't mixed in. I searched the old clock. Nancy Drew lives.

"Maybe there is no ledger," I said to Boone. "Maybe Corny kept everything on his phone."

"He'd have a paper backup. People lose phones, and Corny didn't have a phone on him. Ross thinks the killer took the phone. She wants us to keep her informed if we come across anything else. I'd say the book is on that second floor somewhere. There's too much action with clients and movers on the first. I'll help."

"You are helping. You're keeping a thousand calories off my thighs." I meandered out into the musty hall piled with chairs, little tables, lamps, pictures, and whatever.

"I meant helping a little closer." I spun around to see Boone coming toward me, using his iPhone flashlight and carrying my purse.

"Yellow really isn't your color."

"I thought it brought out the color of my eyes." He handed over the purse.

"You're breaking the law."

"I won't tell if you won't tell, and you're my wife, so all bets are off. Besides, I finished up the mac and cheese and got bored. And the sooner we get out of here, the sooner we can do something that I promise will be very unboring." Boone wagged his brows and added a *come and get me* look that made my stomach flip.

"You take the rooms at the far end and I'll take the kitchen and the other two?"

Boone faded into the dark, his footsteps echoing and old

floorboards moaning. I headed for the kitchen. There were no dishes in the sink and a worn oak chair, and table sat at the window. I opened the freezer to two bottles of gin and a frozen-over ice tray. "I don't think Corny ever cooked in this kitchen."

"That's 'cause he was too busy with his sixty-inch plasma TV and serious cable setup. He has a theater recliner with cupholders in here and an extra AC unit. There's even a mini fridge and ice cube maker. The man knew how to live."

To me, big TVs were like having unwanted roommates in your house. But one can never have too much ice. The scent of burning leaves drifted my way. Nothing smelled better in the fall than burning leaves, except pumpkin pie baking. The next room on my left had a double pedestal dining room table, chairs, and matching credenza. Hutch, couches covered with sheets to protect from dust, end tables and the like crowded the next room. Everything ready for the big move to Jones Street? I checked under, over and in everything finding zilch.

A Tiffany lamp, obviously on a timer, sat on a cherry desk at the end of the hall. Foggy moonlight fell though the clerestory window and spilled over the cherry desk and little Duncan Phyfe chair. I leaned across the desk, trying to see who was burning leaves at this hour, and spotted something wedged between the desk and the wall. I could hear Boone rummaging around in the other room. I scooted out the little chair then the desk, the legs scraping across the worn floorboards. I wiggled free three paintings from behind the desk. One was of a gazebo, the other Forsythe Park, and was that *Golf Is a Many Splendored Thing*? Really? Okay, *maybe* it was *Splendored Thing*. Finding a golf painting in Savannah was like finding fat cherub paintings in Italy: they were everywhere.

I directed my beam at the painting with a lake in the background and geese in V formation overhead. A little red flag with an 18 on it fluttered from that stick thing jammed in the hole. A golfer in a green cap--who I always thought looked like Uncle Putter--stood ready to make the shot.

"Hey, husband, you'll never guess what I found," I said to Boone over the phone. "I got the original of Auntie KiKi's painting." I held it up to the moonlight to get a better look, and a pouch fell from the back, landing on the desk. The pouch was black with "Home Office Security Fireproof" stamped in red. I propped *Splendored Thing* against the chair then unzipped the pouch and pulled out...holy cheese and crackers...a thin book plus a brown envelope.

"Boone, for crying in a bucket, stop channel surfing. I got the ledger." I sat down at the desk and flipped open the book. "From the looks of these numbers," I said as Boone's footsteps sounded behind me, "Corny was making off like a bandit, literally. Look at these columns of initials, next to descriptions and prices, one being much lower than the other. Just like we suspected, Corny reported one price to the customer and sold it for a lot more. Fudging numbers let him launder his bribery money. Look, here's 'ZC 1943 Lincoln, JLC mahogany sideboard, MAH Biedermeier writing desk.' Zelda, JerryLee and Margaret Ann."

I passed the book back to Boone then dumped out the envelope. "Here's Mildred's penny in a plastic cover--who knew a penny could be worth so much? Here're pictures of some paintings including *Splendored Thing,* a diamond ring and necklace, and a wrecked Jeep next to a fence with an April timestamp and--"

Boone grabbed the photos out of my hand.

"Hey! Patience is a virtue." I spun around to piercing eyes staring out from a black hood. An evil laugh split the quiet and my heart stopped dead in my chest. I shoved at Hoodie Guy to get him away then got knocked to the floor with the chair crashing over my head. Gasping as much from sheer terror and a head bashing as the swirling smoke, I struggled to stand.

Hoodie Guy was gone. So were the journal and pictures. Thickening smoke closed in around me.

"Boone!" I coughed and stumbled down the hall past the kitchen. A wall of gray rolled up the stairs with leaping flames close behind. "Boone! Where are you?"

Heat radiated through the floor and into my shoes. My eyes burned, and I tottered into the TV room. Streetlight from outside outlined Boone slumped over the recliner.

"Get up! Get up!" I tried to pull him back, but he was dead weight. No! Not dead! Please not dead. "You are not going to make me a widow, Walker Boone," I sobbed as I rolled him onto the floor. His eyes were closed, he was barely breathing, and blood dripped from his forehead.

"You hear me!" I sobbed more, shaking his shoulders and slapping his face. "Not a widow! I'm a bride! Sexy, voluptuous bride. I will not lose you. This is our honeymoon. I love you." I framed Boone's face between my palms and kissed him hard. His eyes popped open.

"R...Reagan?"

"It worked! Just like in the fairytales." I grabbed the front of Boone's shirt and yanked up with all my might till I got him wedged between the recliner and me. I draped his arm over my shoulder for support.

Sirens sounded in the distance, but a hundred-and-fifty-year-old clapboard crammed with wood furniture was a freaking tinderbox. Smoke curled closer, and fire ate at the doorway behind us. The window was the only way out.

Channeling junior high karate class, I yelled, "Ki-ai!" and side-kicked the AC unit clear out of the window, sending it flying onto the porch roof and somersaulting out of sight. And to think, I only got a C in that class. Using my shoulder, I pried up the window then pushed Boone though like Rabbit did to Pooh. I dove after Boone, skidded down the moss-covered shingles, and grabbed Boone's leg to stop myself from careening off the edge. The fresh air brought Boone alert. Fire roared from behind and columns of black swelled in front.

We exchanged what-now looks just as the roof gave way. I screamed. Boone yelled something guaranteed to put Auntie KiKi in a swoon, and the two of us crashed down onto the wicker settee below, jarring me to the fillings of my teeth.

Boone took my hand and kissed the palm. "I need a beer."

AFTER GIVING AUNTIE KIKI THE SAME SANITIZED VERSION BOONE and I gave the firemen, the police, and Scarlett Rose as to what happened at the auction house...like we saw the place on fire and checked to see if anyone was inside...I hung up the phone. Cocooned in my Hello Kitty nightshirt that wasn't exactly honeymoon attire but oh-so-comforting, I sat cross-legged in the middle of the bed Boone and I had splurged on from Pottery Barn. BW rested his snout on my leg.

Just breathe, I said to myself. I stroked BW and tried to stop shaking. *Boone's fine.* I listened to the rain of shower water echoing from the bathroom. *We're fine.* The water turned off and Boone came out, towel loose at his lean hips, steam flowing behind him.

"You need stitches." My voice wobbled.

Boone touched the butterfly Band-Aid on his forehead. He sat down next to a tray of iced tea and wedding cookies that I'd brought up. He wrapped his arm around me. "It's a scratch."

"A scratch is what you get from a cat, and you were in that house because of me."

"You're not the one who hit me over the head. You didn't start the fire. In fact, you got me out of it."

"You were unconscious." A tear slid down my cheek, and I swiped it away. "You should have gone to the hospital like the

EMS guy said. You could have a concussion. You could be bleeding in your brain, and when you told him you lived next door to a doctor that was a big fat lie."

"My vision, memory, and balance are fine. I have a headache, but it's going away, and I *do* live next door to a doctor."

"He's at a freaking conference! I should call Big Joey. Big Joey would make you go to the hospital. Big Joey could talk some sense into you. Big Joey--"

Boone kissed me, cutting off my rant.

"You can't kiss your way out of this."

"Wanna bet?"

I scooted back out of reach and gave Boone an angry mommy stare that Gloria used on me and that I swore I'd never use. Yet here I was. "I Googled concussion. You are to rest, keep hydrated, and you are not to sleep for three hours."

Boone flashed me a dopey smile.

"And we are not doing *that* for three hours. *That* is not resting!"

"*That* is a lot more fun."

I reached around Boone, grabbed a glass of tea and handed it to him. "Drink."

"You know," Boone said after emptying the glass, "there is something we need to face."

"That this will go down in history as truly the honeymoon from hell?"

"That the fire was arson, and it was personal and not just Corny's house personal."

"Yeah." I scooted close and rested my head on Boone's chest. "We were there."

"*You* were there. It's no secret that you're trying to get KiKi off the hook for Corny's murder. Then you and Miss Anklet show up at Jen's and Friends and ask a bunch of questions in front of a lot of people. Someone wants you out of the way, Sweething.

They want to keep KiKi front and center as the suspect. Someone followed you to the auction house and--"

"And they took the ledger!" I jumped up and faced Boone. "With the fire and you hurt and falling through a roof, I forgot all about the blasted ledger. Everything happened so fast I forgot about it. The ledger was behind the original painting of *Golf Is a Many Splendored Thing.* There was Mildred's penny, and pictures of jewelry, and a wrecked Jeep."

Boone finished off a cookie. "My guess is our arsonist was after the journal. People don't kill over paintings and jewelry, and maybe he liked that Jeep and wrecked it."

Boone strolled over to the dresser and turned off the lamp. "I still have a picture of a midnight-blue '95 Mustang that I got...well, we won't talk about how I got it."

"You were a bad boy, Walker Boone."

"Still am in some ways." Boone snuggled in. "Let me show you." He did a little ear nibble thing, turning my brain to mush...but not completely.

"And-there's-something-else!" I bolted up.

"I think I broke a tooth."

I flipped the lamp back on. "The Sleepy Pines van nearly ran Auntie KiKi and me over tonight at Johnson Square. The waiter guy at Jen's and Friends said old people were celebrating in the back room. I bet it was the Piners winding up for their Vegas trip. Irene Fairbanks could have followed me to IDD and torched the place so I wouldn't find evidence that might implicate someone else. With hoisting wheelchairs and walkers, getting up onto the roof wouldn't be all that hard. We need to talk to Irene." I started for the bedroom door, and Boone snagged my arm.

"It's midnight, Sweething."

"We'll wake her up. She hit you over the head and she clobbered me, and she tried to turn us into crispy critters. And she's a home wrecker. I'll shake that little floozy awake till her bones rattle."

"Very noble, but it's been three hours and seventeen minutes since we fell through the roof." Boone pulled back the covers and patted the pillow. "Maybe Irene can wait till tomorrow?"

CHAPTER 10

"Do you hear knocking?" I mumbled to Boone as the first touch of pearl-gray morning crept into the bedroom.

"Let's pretend we don't."

"It's getting louder." I burrowed farther into the covers. "Could be Mamma. If she heard about the fire, she'd know I was involved. She won't be going away anytime soon."

"She wouldn't knock. She knows where the key is."

I struggled out of bed, trying not to disturb BW and his little doggy snores. I stumbled down the stairs, finger comb my hair--which had to look as if I had stuck my finger in a socket--and tore open the door to, "Aldeen?"

"This morning it's Detective Ross."

"It's five a.m."

"If I don't sleep, nobody sleeps." She gave me an up-and-down look and wrinkled her nose. "Hello Kitty? Seriously? You got the hottest guy east of the Mississippi warming your bed, and you do Hello Kitty? Girl, you need to read one of those Harlequin romance books."

Aldeen pushed inside and handed me one of two cups of

Starbucks. "I need to know what happened at the auction house, and not that bunch of malarkey you fed the on-duty cop last night. Spill it."

"How'd you get so cranky?"

"Comes with the job and interfering citizenry burning down buildings."

"I didn't set that fire, and neither did Boone." I took a sip of no-sugar, no-cream coffee used for blasting brain cells awake. "And if the police start poking around everyone dives for cover. Leads will disappear, and we'll all get nowhere quick in finding out who did what. You need to back off and give me some time."

"Leads?" Aldeen's gaze fused with mine through the dim light. Okay, it was time for a little *I'll tell you if you tell me*. The police had access to databases and info I could never get my hands on. With me operating on the legal fringes, the reverse was true for Aldeen.

"Corny was skimming his clients over antique sales, and that's motive," I offered.

Aldeen gave me a *who cares?* shoulder roll, meaning that was old news. Like Boone said, knocking someone off over an under-priced coffee table wasn't much of a motive.

"Corny was forging paintings," I added. "With Savannah College of Art and Design at our doorstep, getting a student to dupe a painting was easy enough. Maybe a client didn't like paying original money for knocked-off merchandise and got even."

Another shoulder roll.

"Corny cheated his sister out of family inheritance?"

"Boring."

"You guys are good."

"That's why they give us badges and guns." Aldeen took a long drink of coffee.

"Irene Fairbanks works at Sleepy Pines, has had her eye on

my Uncle Putter for years, and is willing to do anything--even frame Auntie KiKi--to get her out of the way. And she didn't like that Corny ripped off the oldsters. That's a two-fer. Get rid of Auntie KiKi *and* avenge the Piners."

That got me an arched left eyebrow. Ah ha! The police didn't know about Irene. Aldeen took another sip of coffee. "Enos had a guy helping him with deliveries."

"So does every other business in Savannah. I give you Irene, and I get a nondescript delivery man?"

"You're lucky I don't haul you in on suspicion of arson. You need to come in and sign a statement about that fire." Aldeen held up her coffee, winked, and walked out the door.

"What was that all about?" Boone wanted to know. He drew up beside me and took a sip of my coffee.

"I need to buy sexy lingerie."

Boone laughed deep in his throat. "Waste of good money when it's just going to wind up on the floor next to the bed."

With both of us now wideawake, Boone volunteered for police station duty with Aldeen, and I'd take on Mamma. I could call or text that I was okay, but "not dead" seemed best delivered in person. Plus, if I showed her the bruise on my shoulder, she might serve up oh-you-poor-thing chocolate chip pancakes.

Boone dropped BW and me off by Oglethorpe Square then sped off toward Bull Street. Joggers in bright spandex sprinted past the fountain, and dog walkers with poopy plastic bags in hand roamed the grassy area. This morning, BW and I were part of the plastic-bag set. Early-morning traffic twined around the cobblestone streets, and a delivery truck at Zunzi's unloaded restaurant supplies. Just like I told Ross: everyone had delivery people.

After the plastic-bag undertaking, BW and I crossed York Street, heading for Mamma's house. The cottage was built for Archibald Bulloch, and that the living room still had three Revolutionary War musket balls embedded in the ceiling made the house truly part of the Historic Landmark District. Mamma's Caddy was parked half at the curb with front wheels on the sidewalk. I opened the picket gate to the pristine white clapboard house where I lived till Hollis swept me off my feet, and I eventually landed in a pile of manure.

To be fair, college Hollis was a sweet guy, the guy I fell in love with. Then he took over his father's real estate business, got bit big-time by the money bug and never recovered. On his business card it read *Anything for a Buck*. Okay, it didn't, but it should have.

I took the brick walk past the stone birdbath and rapped the brass pineapple knocker, the true symbol of Southern hospitality. Nothing. I gave it another rap. Still nothing. It was too early for court. Church? That was a possibility, considering her sister was arrested for murder and her one and only beloved daughter nearly barbecued. I punched #2 speed-dial on Flippy, and Mamma picked up. "Hey," I said. "I'm outside your house."

"Hey, I'm not inside." Mamma giggled, or was that crying? "I'm around the corner at 212 Oglethorpe." She disconnected.

She was so worried and distraught about me maybe being hurt that she went to a friend's house? Good grief! It was truly touching that she cared so much.

I closed the gate behind BW, my hand stopping on the latch. Where had I seen this fence, other than the bazillion times I'd painted it? The Jeep in the photograph! Corny crashed his beloved Jeep into a fence? Why keep a picture of that? BW and I crossed York and headed for Oglethorpe. I counted off the addresses of big houses with late-summer roses, stately columns, and fancy balustrades. I took the wrought-iron stairs up to the veranda and the red, six-panel front door. I gave the pineapple knocker a rap, and the door flew open to... "Judge Swain?"

"Mornin', Reagan. I'm glad you're looking so well."

"I'm...I'm glad you're looking so well too."

"I...we...Gloria and I heard on the news about the fire at the auction house. That Scarlett Rose reporter said it was arson, but everyone got out okay. Your mother was concerned you might be involved. She came over here to...uh...talk about it, and would you care to join us for breakfast?"

Us? Breakfast?

"Coffee. And maybe I was a little involved," I added to fill the silence. Plus, sooner or later, my name would be attached to the fire. I ratcheted up my innocent smile and entered the hallway with brass chandelier, curved staircase, and BW's nails taping on the polished hardwood floor.

"You see," I rambled on, "Boone and I were walking by the I Do Declare auction house, and lo and behold, it was on fire of all things. We went in just to make sure no one was there."

The kitchen was big and modern with a low fire glowing in the hearth. Mamma was in a robe and sitting at a lovely round mahogany table. She came up beside the judge, and he relaxed, giving me a lopsided grin. "Really? That's the best you can do?"

"It was the 'lo and behold,' wasn't it? Too over the top? I'm never my best in the morning." *Especially this morning.* What was Mamma doing at Swain's house? And that was without a doubt the most stupid question I'd ever asked in my entire life.

I took a seat at the table, and were those chocolate chip pancakes, *my* chocolate chip pancakes, stacked on two plates? And crispy bacon? And a bottle of maple syrup?

"Any new suspects on who did in Corny?" Swain retrieved a mug from the cabinet then poured out coffee. "I've been doing a little asking around." He joined Mamma and me at the table. "It seems Corny was skimming money from antique sales. That might be something to go on."

I took a sip of coffee. "This is really good. Mamma, usually your coffee is..." *dishwater,* I added to myself then said, "Different."

"That's because the one who made the coffee is different." Mamma winked at Swain, he cut into his pancakes, and I nearly slid off my chair.

"And there's Irene Fairbanks," I said to get my mind off *different.* "She works at Sleepy Pines and has a soft spot for the residents who Corny double-crossed. She has a really big soft spot for my uncle. And then there's Corny's sister, who's getting married. Now she can get her inheritance and afford the wedding she planned. Corny had pictures of forged paintings and a crunched Jeep with a little yellow decal on the driver's side. I forgot about the decal. Maybe a gym membership?"

"Or a resident on-street city parking permit." Mamma picked up a strip of bacon. "Red is for this area. I think Walker's is green."

Judge Swain's eyes rounded over his last forkful of pancakes with little drops of thick golden maple syrup dripping from the edges. "That is a lot of suspects, and if one of them really is the killer, you should be careful. He or she won't hesitate to do it again."

"You don't have to worry about the Summerside women. We're a sturdy lot." Mamma flipped her hair and flashed a dopey grin.

"But I do worry." Swain put down his fork, and this time my eyes rounded. How could he not finish off every morsel of chocolate chip pancakes?

"We've been together a few months now," Swain said. "We're family. Nothing is more important to me than that." He wiped his mouth with a napkin, stood and kissed Mamma on the cheek. "I better get a move on. I have court this morning. See you at seven for dinner?"

"Perfect." And from the look on Mamma's face, she meant it.

The judge's steps echoed down the hall. Mamma sighed and fed BW the spoon from the sugar bowl. I retrieved the spoon and fed BW the judge's last bite of pancake. "This is a beautiful house," I said to fill the quiet.

Mamma reached over my mug, snagged the little pitcher of cream, gave it a quick stir, then drank down the contents. "You know," she said, her eyes dreamy, "Everett restored it top to bottom. He did much of the carpentry work himself. There's something about a man working with tools that's so appealing. Not that I need a man in my life, mind you." Mamma squared her shoulders, a little of the dreamy fading. "I'm perfectly fine on my own, have been all these years, and there's no need to change now, though..."

Mamma let out another sigh. "He does have a lovely smile, and those little laugh lines at the corner of his deep-brown eyes sure make my heart go pitty-pat. And that hair." Mamma took another drink of the cream. "He certainly has lovely hair."

Pitty-pat? Had Mamma ever said pitty-pat in her life? "So, tell me, how's that cup of coffee?"

"Delightful, dear, just delightful. Is there some particular reason you stopped by?"

Like Cher says, *If grass can grow through cement, love can find you at every time in your life.* "Just happened to be in the neighborhood."

BW and I headed for the hall. We passed the living room with cream sofas, expensive lamps, an antique desk that Louis-the-whatever would be proud to use, and a wall of family photos professionally framed and arranged.

I closed the door behind me and took the steps to the sidewalk as a black Caddy rolled to a stop at the curb. The window powered down to Judge Swain. "Can we talk for a few minutes? I can give you a lift to your house."

"A guy in a black hoodie with an alligator burned down the auction house. I didn't do it."

"And your mother didn't come over to talk about the fire."

I put BW in the backseat, took the front, and the judge hit the gas. "I want you to know that I really care about Gloria. I'm not just playing fast and loose with her affections, and I know that KiKi means a lot to her. I want to help find KiKi innocent."

Swain took a right onto Whittaker. "What if I check the inheritance situation on McBride's sister and see just how much money is involved? You said something about a woman who works at the Pines being a suspect. We can both talk to her. If she knew about the deed to Rosegate, she could have used the situation to her advantage to frame KiKi."

Swain gave me a little smile. "I was a litigator, and I can be very persuasive in getting the truth out of people. You see...uh, well, I want your mother to like me. If I can assist you with getting your auntie found innocent of all charges, that would be a feather in my cap, so to speak."

"Best I can tell, you have lots of feathers already. When it comes to Mamma, you're a step away from being a full-fledged duck. And you should know, or maybe not know, that some of the stuff I get involved in well... It's best if you didn't know. Not that I exactly break the law," I rushed on, "but I've been known to sidestep it once in a while. You're the law and that's what's important or there'd be nothing but chaos around here and— Holy cow!" I pointed out the windshield. "There's the Sleepy Pines van with Irene Freemont at the wheel. She's driving like a maniac, and there's no one else in the van."

"She's sure going somewhere in a hurry. She ran that light onto Oglethorpe, and she just missed hitting that bus." Swain glanced at me out of the corner of his eye. "You think she knows you're on to her? Maybe she's making a run for it? Maybe she realizes she's in over her head?" The judge smacked his palm against the steering wheel. "I'm going to follow that van." He laughed, his eyes crinkling at the corners like Mamma said.

Swain hit the gas hard, making me realize why people pay the big bucks for high-performance cars. I grabbed the middle console out of habit from driving with Mamma, and my hand landed next to mail with Final Notice stamped in red across the front.

"Look," Swain said, nodding up ahead. "She's taking Martin Luther and the cutoff for I-16."

"The airport!"

"That's what I would do." Swain gave me a sly smile. "This is kind of fun."

"If we get caught for speeding, it's not going to be fun for you."

"I'll tell the cops it's all your fault." The smile morphed into a full grin, and when I looked back to the console the mail was gone.

Swain did some fancy weaving in and out of traffic. "I better not get too close," he said, snapping my attention back to the chase. "She'll know we're tailing her. She's in the right lane for I-95. Definitely the airport."

Normally, it was about a thirty-minute ride to Savannah International. On so many levels, there was not one thing normal about this ride. "You're really a good driver."

"All that Mario Kart paid off. She's taking the airport exit, all right."

We followed the van to the ramp marked Departures, and Irene screeched to the curb. Swain tried to double-park next to the van but got cut off by a taxi. I craned my neck to keep watch. "She's hauling a bunch of luggage out of the back and tossing it on the sidewalk! She is so making a run for it!"

"Not on my watch, she's not." Swain pulled to a stop behind a red SUV.

BW and I jumped out of the car with me waving my arms and both of us running. "You're not getting away, Irene. Stop! We got you now." I snagged the suitcase Irene had in her hand and tugged with all my might. Irene had better might and pulled it free. Swain ran up beside me as the orange-vested airport security trotted over. BW sat down, tail wagging, and waited for a pat and treat. BW was many things, but canine pursuit dog was not one of them.

"What in blazes is going on here?" The red-faced security guard pointed to the three of us. "And that mutt needs to be on a leash!"

"Mutt? Mutt!" I growled. "You're the one who needs to be on a--"

Swain grabbed my arm and pulled me back. "I'm a judge here in Savannah." Swain drew himself up straight and tall, looking very judgelike. "This woman is a murder suspect. She's trying to flee the country, and I'm here to set things right."

Irene's head snapped back, and she looked from me to Swain. "You two are out of your pea-picking minds. I'm not going anywhere. This isn't *my* luggage, you idiots. It's theirs." Irene nodded to five women trotting toward her, one wearing a white baseball cap with *Bride* in pink sequins across the front.

"I took these gals to the airport this morning," Irene went on, "and they forgot half their bloomin' luggage. Happens a lot when people spend more time bachelorette partying than packing. Anyway, I was bringing them their stuff and they need to catch their flights right now or I'll get a bad review on Yelp and I sure can't have that."

Irene handed the suitcases over to the disheveled, obviously hungover thirty-somethings who would no doubt look a lot better on the wedding day. They handed Irene a wad of bills and trotted back into the airport entrance with their luggage bouncing along behind them.

"Well, they sure aren't the Piners. What's going on?" I pointed to the van while onlookers gathered.

Irene parked her fist on her hip. "I run an Uber on the side, that's what's going on. Hauling old folks around barely puts a roof over my head, and they can't afford to pay me more. So I do a little compensating. I might be guilty of using this here van to make a few bucks, but as for murder--and I assume you're talking about old Corny--there's no way on God's green earth I could have knocked him off, even though I sure would have liked to. That pipsqueak had it coming. I was with Mildred Heatherweight at the hospital. I happened to be there Friday night sort of visiting a friend when they brought her in. She had a heart attack that turned out not to be a sugar rush from a cotton candy martini at Jen's and Friends. She needed a friendly face, so I hung around."

"You were at the hospital stalking my Uncle Putter."

"That's it!" The guard held out his arms. "I don't care if she was stalking Santa Claus, and I don't give a flying fig who any of you are." The cop glared directly at Swain. "You all need to get your cars, your butts, and your mangy mutt out of my airport before I have you towed and cited and put in the pound where you belong. Got it!"

The security guard turned and tripped over a suitcase, landing face down, proving beyond a shadow of a doubt that the good Lord above was indeed a dog lover. Irene flipped an unmistakable hand gesture then climbed back in the van. Swain, BW and I headed for the Caddy.

"I'm sorry I pulled you into this," I said to Swain while we drove out of the airport. "My reputation with the police is mostly *what has she done this time*? But considering the crowd we drew, I'm sure our encounter will be all over your courtroom, and that can't be good for your reputation."

Swain looked at me then barked out a laugh. "Sorry? It feels good to get involved in a case and see things from the other side for a change. Gets kind of stuffy sitting up there on that bench, and truth be told, I don't recall you pulling me into anything. It was more the other way around. And the way I see it, this wasn't all for naught. Now we know that Irene has an alibi, and we can take her off the suspect list. I just wonder what your mother's going to say when she gets wind of our little adventure. Think she'll be mad at me?"

"She'll be mad at *me* for involving you, and maybe she'll be mad at you too. Mostly because you didn't bring her along."

CHAPTER 11

"So, wife, how are things out at the airport this fine morning?" Boone wanted to know.

BW and I walked up the sidewalk after Swain had dropped us off. I sat down next to Boone on our front porch that soon wouldn't be our front porch.

"How'd you know?"

"For the Savannah kudzu vine, it's been Christmas morning and the Fourth of July all rolled into one." Boone pulled out his iPhone and scrolled the screen. "These are but a few of the texts, phone messages, and let's not forget Facebook and Instagram shots that I got in the last hour. The security cop flat on the tarmac outdid you on likes and shares."

"Mamma's going to throw a hissy that Swain was involved, and she is not for one minute going to believe this was all his idea."

"I got a hard time believing that one. The only thing saving you is that our favorite female judge is one lovestruck lady. I stopped at her house, thinking you might need a ride home, and saw her car parked at the curb and surrounding area. Maybe I should drive her to the courthouse this afternoon? The

Summerside name has occupied the Savannah headlines enough lately without adding an accident report."

"There's something else."

"You're now on the no-fly list?"

"When I was in Swain's car, I saw mail marked Final Notice."

"So he misplaced some bills. We've all done it. I haven't heard any rumblings about Swain and money problems. I can have Big Joey make inquiries."

"I don't want Mamma to think I'm making waves. You're right, it was probably an oversight. But all this wasn't a complete waste of time. We found out that Irene Fairbanks has a foolproof alibi for the night of the murder." I took a bite of Boone's bagel that would taste a lot better if it were a sprinkle doughnut. "Uncle Putter."

"Clandestine affair?"

"Restraining order violation." I fed a chunk of bagel to BW. "That leaves us with Emmilene and the Jeep picture."

"Ross said Enos was grooming his nephew to take over the auction house. I doubt if he welcomed Corny with open arms, so that's another suspect."

"All Aldeen told me was that Enos had a delivery guy."

"I bought Cakery Bakery doughnuts and coffee for the station house." Boone planted a soft kiss on my lips. "We didn't find Corny's Jeep at IDD. If it was involved in his illegal activities, he would have gotten rid of it in the river or some junkyard. But it's worth a shot to look around. If we do find it, it could lead us to someone else who Corny had in his clutches."

"Enos will be at the wake this evening. We can ask him about his nephew." I started to laugh. "Junkyards and wakes. And to think some people go to Hawaii for a honeymoon."

Boone headed off to collect Mamma and save Savannah from more Summerside chaos. BW and I opened the Fox. Two of my regulars out to score a deal hustled in the door along with a stream of newbie customers. No doubt they were here to check out the bride who found a body under her cake table and had a run-in with airport police. Adding to the little parade was Hollis, hoisting yet another crate of whatever. He parked it on the counter, wiped sweat from his forehead, and added a snort.

"A burning building followed by airport security on your case, that's over the top even for the likes of Reagan Summerside."

"Keep your stuff to one side of the kitchen so it doesn't get mixed in with the furniture, okay?"

"When are you going to start moving that stuff? You're running out of time, you know." Hollis gazed around the Fox with lust in his eyes. "Can't wait to start decorating. Wait till you see what I brought over this time."

Hollis yanked out a flag folded into one of those glass triangle display cases. "Dad had a military funeral, and I'm going to mount this on the wall in the entrance hall."

He dumped out a tin of medals. "Found the dog tags in the bottom of my mamma's old jewelry box. Gonna put all these in shadow boxes and hang 'em beside the family crest."

"Since when do the Beaumonts have a family crest?"

"Since I learned Photoshop." Hollis cut his gaze to the open front door. "Good criminy, here come the wake warblers all dressed in black mourning weeds. Living next to them is going to be creepy. Maybe I can pull some strings now that I have clout in this city and get the three of them tossed out of the neighborhood."

Three? I did a double take. Elsie, Annie Fritz, and... "You got to be kidding."

"Yeah, that's what I say every time I see those old biddies around town." Hollis scooped everything backing the crate and headed for the kitchen,

I stage-whispered to sister number three as she walked in the door, "What do you think you're doing?"

Auntie KiKi stuck out her lower lip and narrowed her eyes. "I'm not getting left out again, that's what I'm doing. Princess is riding around on that Roomba vacuum thing with my ankle monitor. I am not getting stuck at home no matter what. A fire? A car chase? Decking the security guy? All the while I'm twiddling my thumbs at home."

"We didn't deck anyone."

"If I was there, we sure enough would have."

Elsie put her arm around Auntie KiKi. "Sister and I came up with a humdinger of a plan. KiKi here is going to sing with us tonight at Corny's wake. The real killer's bound to show up, and maybe we can figure out who it is. KiKi's already got this here black dress that blends in right nice with our funeral attire. All we need is a hat."

Lord, take me now. "Have you ever heard this woman sing? Think cat in heat."

Auntie KiKi narrowed her brows. "I'll have you know that my voice is plum terrific."

"For a cat in heat."

"It's a funeral," Elsie jumped in. "It's supposed to sound sad, and it's the least we can do. KiKi helped Sister and me stay out of the pokey. We're just returning the favor, is all. Tonight, it's the trio of Elsie, Annie Fritz and ..."

"Bambi," Auntie Kiki offered and fluffed her hair. "Always wanted to be a hot little number named Bambi."

The three of us, along with BW, stared at KiKi and Elise said, "You cannot have a hooker name for a wake. You're MaryLouise, and now we need the hat. We always wear hats, and a big one will cover MaryLouise's face--"

"And hopefully her mouth," I added under my breath.

"I heard that," Auntie KiKi huffed and Elsie continued, "It's the perfect plan. No one will recognize KiKi tonight, not like now when anyone who comes along--"

"I have to sell this here wedding dress," Emmilene blurted from the doorway. Sniffing and wiping her eyes, she shuffled inside, elbowed Elsie out of the way, and dropped a white garment bag on the counter right in front of Auntie Kiki. Emmilene unzipped the bag.

"Never wore the dress, and the only reason I'm here talking to you, the niece of that horrible woman who lives next door and murdered my dearly departed and oh-so-loving brother, is that I need to pay for his funeral."

Auntie KiKi, Annie Fritz, and Elsie didn't move a muscle. Emmilene let out an ear-piercing wail that sent BW diving under the checkout desk and customers scurrying out the door. "I'd like nothing more than to get my hands on KiKi Vanderpool and wring her little old neck!"

"Well now, I don't know about her being all that old," Auntie KiKi said while staring straight ahead. "I heard she's kind of a looker."

I shoved a box of tissues across the counter to get Emmilene's attention while Annie Fritz and Elsie hooked arms though Auntie Big Mouth and trotted her toward the hat rack.

Emmilene turned and pointed. "Wait! I know you."

The sisters plus Auntie KiKi froze, and little dots danced before my eyes. This was it. This was Emmilene recognizing Auntie KiKi, calling the cops and getting KiKi sent back to jail.

Emmilene squinted, blinked and looked again. "I...I hired you to sing at my brother's wake this evening," she said, more to herself than anyone else. "But now there're...there're three of you?"

"We're having a sale." Elsie turned and flashed a smile. "Three for the price of two so we sound extra good."

"This is a really nice dress," I said to Emmilene to get her focus on me and not the warblers. "But not designer quality."

"I'm upgrading." Emmilene kept staring at the three sisters. "My new dress is from Mary Elizabeth's Boutique. Had to buy off-the-rack on short notice and have it altered. The wedding is at the country club with Claude Monet roses and hydrangeas and not cheap yellow and white mums that some people have."

"I do a fifty-fifty split after the dress sells."

Emmilene's attention darted back to me. "That's highway robbery."

"So are utility bills, taxes, loan payment, and insurance." I slid the new customer account agreement, plus pen, at Emmilene, and told her what to read and sign. I power-walked over to Auntie KiKi. I grabbed her hand and hauled her plus big black hat toward the kitchen.

"What's with all these boxes back here?" she asked.

This was not the time to spring the great Cherry House swap on Auntie KiKi, so I went with "Some old stuff I'm getting rid of, and you need to get out of here right now. I think Emmilene might have recognized you."

"Honey, the only thing that girl recognizes is dollar signs. If she knew who I was, she'd have called the cops by now. See you at the Slumber. I'll be the sexy singer in the middle."

Auntie KiKi kissed my cheek and darted out the door, and when I got back to the counter, the sisters and Emmilene were gone. Little black dress business at the Prissy Fox was in full swing for the rest of the day. Funerals were big in Savannah, especially with talk of an open casket and the amount of putty used to fill in the dead guy's dented head.

At five sharp I closed up shop and headed upstairs to slink into a little black dead dress of my own, which I saved for just such occasions. Wearing it anyplace else always put a damper on the evening. Boone was already in the apartment dressed in gray slacks and white shirt. He had a dishtowel at his waist and something delicious simmering on the stove. I grabbed a quick kiss that ended up being not so quick then sat down at the table and dug into chicken with wild rice and broccoli. I could have done without the broccoli.

"This is really good," I said around a mouthful while feeding a chunk of chicken to BW.

Boone looked at me over a forkful of rice. "As good as SpaghettiO surprise?"

"Nothing's as good as my SpaghettiO surprise."

"I'm baking brownies for dessert."

"You win." I plucked up a broccoli spear and bit off the top. "Any luck with the Jeep?"

"Corny either sold it, or he ditched it."

I ate two more bites to ward off scurvy and rotting bones, then gazed across the table to my wonderful husband. "He cooks and he's good in bed. Am I a lucky girl or what?"

"How about I prove that last part, so you don't forget." Boone stalked around the table and swept me up in a big hug. He nuzzled my neck, then nuzzled lower, leaving us with ruined brownies and being an hour late for Corny's funeral.

"LOOK HOW FAR BACK WE ARE IN THE RECEIVING LINE," I whispered to Boone when we finally got to House of Eternal Slumber. The din of Broad Street traffic faded behind us, and we hurried up the sidewalk. Evening shadows fell across the lush landscape and manicured lawn while chandelier light spilled from the big arched windows. The old antebellum now funeral parlor--with original widow's walk on top and embalming rooms in back—was the Ritz-Carlton for Savannah's dearly departed.

"Half the city must be here, and the line's out the door. At this rate, we'll never get inside to have a look around." I drew up close to Boone. "And I think people are staring at us."

"That Corny was an uninvited guest at our wedding might have something to do with the staring, but I wonder why Aldeen Ross is here?" Boone nodded to a woman in a big black hat with a white feather who stood near the front of the line. "I doubt if she and Corny were pals. She's wearing gym shoes, and even I know feathers and gym shoes don't mix. Aldeen Ross is in cop mode. She's here for a reason, and she's looking for something."

"Or someone. Guess who's singing with the Abbott sisters tonight at the wake, and I'll give you a clue: it's not Adele."

"Ankle monitor?"

"It hitched a ride on a Roomba. I got to get Auntie KiKi out of the Slumber before Aldeen gets in there. The next time she looks away, I'll duck into the bushes and cut around to the back entrance."

Boone handed me the keys to the Chevy. "No stopping for doughnuts."

"But we burnt the brownies."

Traffic on Broad purred along at an unnervingly calm pace. Where was a fender bender when you really needed one? The white feather inched closer to the double glass doors, and I bit off two fingernails. In desperation, I made the sign of the cross.

"What are you doing?"

"Praying for a little mayhem."

"Are you allowed to do that?"

"Mayhem is my life. I'm just asking to rearrange the timing." I added an *amen* as a fire truck with flashing lights and siren rounded the corner. Boone's jaw dropped a fraction in total astonishment, and Aldeen snapped her head toward the street. I held tight to Old Yeller--that didn't go all that well with my dead dress--and ducked behind two hydrangeas.

Staying in the shadows, I followed the sidewalk to the back

parking lot just as a black Jeep zipped past. There were a lot of black Jeeps in Savannah, and Corny's could be anywhere. If Boone couldn't find it, it was no doubt sitting at the bottom of the Savannah River. I pushed open the door marked Receiving and entered a hallway of muted lighting, thick carpeting, and an off-key version of "How Great Thou Art" drifting my way.

"Mercedes?" I whispered. She had to be around somewhere in case the dead needed a last-minute touchup. Too much putty and rouge and the deceased looked plastic, too little and they looked...dead. And then there were those who felt the need to kiss the deceased goodbye, really messing things up. Oh, the stuff I've learned from having a mortician beautician as a bestie. "Mercedes?"

I stepped farther into the hallway lined with doors labeled Cosmetology, Display, Repository, Embalming. The overpowering scent of flowers and burning candles closed in around me, along with the eerie feeling of not being alone. "M...Mercedes?"

"What?"

I jumped, fell against the wall, slid to the floor, and passed out. Okay, I didn't pass out, but it was touch and go there for a second. "How do you work in this place?"

"I show up, do my magic, they pay me and it's a darn good thing you're here." Mercedes pulled off her apron splotched with makeup and was that hair dye? Lord, please let it be hair dye.

"KiKi," Mercedes continued, "can't sing for beans, and no one's going to hire Elsie and Annie Fritz ever again if you don't do something right quick to get KiKi out of here. I thought she was sequestered at her house."

"So did the police, and now Aldeen Ross is right outside the door, waiting to pay her respects."

"Does anyone ever stay home in this city?" Mercedes grabbed my hand, and we trotted down the hallway. Mercedes's ample girth easily outhustled me with every step. We pulled up to the back entrance of the Pastoral Garden room, least that's what the plaque said. House of Eternal Slumber was big on signage. Brocade drapes hung at the windows, maroon carpet covered the pine floors, and sisters-three hummed the intro to "When We Gather at the River." The tea table-- aka ground zero for all things gossip--was positioned between upholstered chairs and sofas. The line of mourners and morbidly curious queued up to the open casket.

"You can wiggle between the row of ferns and come up behind KiKi that way," Mercedes whispered. "With Corny not missed by one and all, the only flowers are the ones Emmilene brought. We had to fill in with artificial foliage kept on hand for our underappreciated guests. You're on your own from here on. I need to be getting back to old Miss Jenkins in cosmetology. She's counting on me to do her roots before tomorrow's viewing."

"Better than embalming."

"Girl, there's not enough money in all Christendom to get me in that room." Mercedes nodded at the casket. "Looks like Davis convinced Emmilene to take a break from dead duty and leave JerryLee in charge. All that talk of 'Doesn't he look nice' takes a toll on the bereaved though I got to admit Corny's some of my best work."

"Davis?"

"Emmilene's fiancé. Seems like a right nice guy."

Mercedes faded into the dim hallway, and Ross and her white feather stepped into the foyer. The singing behind me lowered in volume but improved in tone, and I cut my eyes to the sisters two.

Where was Auntie KiKi? Why did Davis sound familiar? And where did that blasted white feather wander off to?

CHAPTER 12

I hurried toward the ferns trying to look as if I wasn't hurrying since no one hurried at a funeral. I got yanked down behind a plastic ficus. "What in blazes is Aldeen Ross doing here?" KiKi panted. "And where did she get that spiffy hat with the feather? I think I need one of those. After all, the only thing that separates us from the animals is our ability to accessorize."

"If we don't get you out of here fast, Ross will accessorize you with a pair of bright shiny handcuffs." I peeked around the ficus. "She's by the casket." I took Auntie KiKi's hand, and we slunk behind two tall men chatting then angled off toward the cookie display, with KiKi snagging a ginger windmill.

"The cookies are stale."

"You're leaving crumbs, and Ross just passed the ficus. Do you think she saw us? Lordy, I bet she saw us. Pull your hat down." We flattened against the wall then inched our way into the back hallway.

"The feather's bobbing our way." Auntie KiKi squeezed my hand. "It's by the table and she's closing in fast. Do something."

"*You* do something."

"I am. I'm stress eating."

I yanked Auntie KiKi into the nearest room, eased the door closed and held the latch so it wouldn't make a loud click when it fell into place.

"Where are we?" KiKi's whisper echoed in the dark room. "Smells funny in here."

"Don't-turn-on-the-light. It...uh...might shine under the door." *And two women screaming their heads off when they realized where they really were would be a dead giveaway.* Dead? Really? "It's just a room," I said in a steady voice, "Where...where...where they store flowers."

"Well, these here flowers smell like that shriveled-up frog I had in biology class when I was in high school and... Reagan," Auntie KiKi's voice dropped two octaves. "Tell me we aren't where I think we are."

"We are in the flower room," I said with a lot more conviction than I felt. I grabbed Auntie KiKi's hand and aimed us toward a red Exit sign glowing from the other side. "Nothing but a little ol' flower room."

"Right." Auntie KiKi's voice wobbled a tad. "Flower room with exotic, weird-smelling flowers. Orchids maybe."

"Yes, orchids. That's it."

We reached the door, I said a quick prayer to any saint on duty, then pushed hard. KiKi and I stumbled out into the sweet-smelling night air. We sprinted for the Chevy parked in the back row, KiKi's hat flapping with each step. We jumped in, and I cranked the mighty engine then gunned all six-hundred horses toward Broad Street.

Auntie KiKi reached into the bosom of her black dress and slid out a little silver flask. She took a long gulp then passed the flask to me. "We were in the--"

"I know." We stopped for a light on Price, and I snuck a swallow of very fine Kentucky bourbon. "And we will never speak of that room again. Did you see any likely suspects hanging around at the funeral?"

"Ronald and Daisy Ballard had smiles on their faces, so I suspect he's taking those little blue pills again. Dorothy Hendricks was making goo-goo eyes at Barney Philpot, so I suspect her divorce from Harvey is final, and she's lookin' for meal ticket number two. And I suspect no one recognized me. I was right worried that Emmilene might after the wedding dress episode at the Fox."

I hung a right on Gwinett and stopped in front of Rosegate. "Get inside, and for the love of all that's holy, please put on that anklet and keep it there. I'll park the Chevy in the garage. In case Aldeen stops by we don't need to be looking as if we just arrived."

Auntie KiKi closed the car door, said she'd have three olive martinis ready and waiting, then trotted up the sidewalk. I pulled into the alley dotted with homeowner cars including yet another big black Jeep with a green Savannah parking sticker and a left crunched bumper. I had to stop obsessing over every car with J-e-e-p on the grill.

I parked the Chevy in the garage, locked up, then texted Boone that Auntie Chicken was in the coop. I snagged my purse out of the back seat and headed for Rosegate. Crickets chirped their final songs of summer, and the first hit of crisp fall air settled around me. I entered the back door and stopped. Why weren't the lights on? Why wasn't Princess standing on the kitchen table hissing at me? No lights and no hissing weren't that alarming but no martinis?

I kept the door open to let in the moonlight and took my phone and flashlight from my purse. I put Old Yeller on the kitchen table and crept into the hallway, voices coming from the living room. Streetlight cut through the front window, silhouetting Auntie KiKi with hands raised over her head. She said something about a delivery, and I didn't catch the rest, because the hum of a motor crept up next to me.

What the heck? I looked down, but not fast enough, and tripped over Princess. My left foot caught the edge of the blasted Roomba, and I stumbled face first to the floor. Princess screeched like the banshee from hell then tore for the kitchen. My phone and flashlight skittered across the hardwood floor, fading into the dark. We should have stayed in the embalming room.

"Who's there?" came a man's voice. "Come out now with your hands up, or I'm blasting this old bat to kingdom come."

"Don't do that." I hobbled into the living room, catching a glint of light reflecting off the barrel of the shotgun.

"Are you okay?" I asked Auntie KiKi.

"You ruined my vacuum, I got called old yet again, and Emmilene and this man are in my house, holding my shotgun. How do you think I am? I told them the painting isn't worth a dime, but they're not listening. Why would anyone want to steal a worthless painting?"

The guy let out an evil laugh, and every hair on my body stood straight up. I knew that laugh. And I knew that black hoodie with a little alligator.

"They realize the painting's a fake," I said to Auntie KiKi. "You bought the original from Enos. Davis here, who happens to be Enos's nephew, made the forgery switch, and now he wants it back. Corny knew about the switch and was blackmailing him. Get rid of Corny, get rid of the evidence a IDD, get the pictures back, and Davis is home free."

Davis pointed the shotgun at me. "Corny's the one who made the forgery switch. That's how he could threaten to tell everyone Enos was selling forgeries. He set him up."

"And my lousy brother said if I took him to court to get my

inheritance, he'd tell everyone Davis was part of the forgery scheme with Enos."

"You were here when Corny was murdered," I said, trying to put together the pieces. "You knew I had mums at my wedding, and there were rose petals in the hall and on the rug around Corny. They were pink like the rose you wear in your hair. You torched IDD to get rid of evidence of the original paintings and the photo of your Jeep that you used for the deliveries. It's parked out in the alley right now."

Davis held up his hand. "What Jeep picture? We had nothing to do with that fire. All we needed was to just get rid of the forgeries. We got the ones from the women at Sleep Pines. I was helping Emmilene with flowers for a wedding party at Jen's and Friends when we saw KiKi. We knew about your wedding, people would be coming and going, and figured it was a good time to get Splendored Thing. We found Corny on the floor with a bashed-in head and a cat sitting on his chest. We heard KiKi coming before we could get the picture, and we ran."

"Or you saw Auntie KiKi in the park and framed her for Corny's murder. Get rid of both of them at one time and get your inheritance. Being president of the Garden Club would be a real boon to your floral shop."

"The only thing you'll ever be president of is Liars Unanimous," Auntie KiKi said. "You don't grow those flowers you have in your shop. I've seen that weed patch you call a garden."

I kicked Auntie KiKi's foot. "This may not be the best time to poke the bear," I said out of the side of my mouth and nodded toward the shotgun.

"Well, you can't go and kill us both now can you." Auntie KiKi folded her arms. "I mean, two dead bodies are a little hard to explain, don't you think?"

"So...so we'll shoot Reagan," Emmilene huffed. "It'll look like you shot her as an intruder. You couldn't live with that, and you turned the shotgun on yourself."

"Actually, that's a pretty darn good story," Auntie KiKi said, adding a few nods. "My expertise with a shotgun is legendary."

"What!" I gasped.

Emmilene shoved the shotgun toward Davis and said, "Do it."

Davis shoved the shotgun back at Emmilene. "Hey, this was your idea. You're the one who said she wouldn't be here, that she was singing with the Abbott sisters."

Emmilene shoved again. "You're the man of the house. You do it."

"This isn't my house."

"No one's shooting anybody," Aldeen boomed from the hallway. She had two police officers at her side, feathered hat slightly askew and Princess snuggled in her arms. Snuggled? Really?

"We tracked KiKi's anklet sprinting down Abercorn," Aldeen said. "Either she had two Red Bulls for dinner, or something was amiss." Aldeen nodded to the officers. "Take the shotgun before somebody gets hurt."

"There's no reason to worry your pretty little heads about that shotgun," KiKi said adding a laugh. "I emptied both barrels at Corny's bony behind when I shooed him out of here, and I never got around to reloading. That's why I was being a little sassy."

"A little!"

"I knew," Auntie KiKi continued, "that I could get away with it. Maybe coax a confession out of these two."

Before any of us understood what was going on, Auntie KiKi wrestled the shotgun away from Davis, aimed at the ceiling, pulled the trigger and blew a hole the size of Atlanta straight into the plaster overhead.

Princess bolted for the door, Aldeen let out a string of expletives, and Auntie KiKi stared at me through a chalky white haze. "You know, now that I think about it, maybe I just emptied *one* of those barrels."

"YOU'VE BEEN STARING AT THAT SPRINKLE DOUGHNUT FOR FIFTEEN minutes," Boone said to me over the rim of his coffee mug. "It's a beautiful fall morning, there's enough evidence that the DA should have a good case against Emmilene and Davis, and KiKi's off the hook--except for another hole in her ceiling. And there's the little matter of her hiding Corny's body, though that's yet to be proved. You should be smiling at your new husband and scarfing sprinkles. What's up?"

I plucked a pink sprinkle off the doughnut and licked it from my thumb. "Cherry House. It's our home."

Boone put down his mug. "What if I call the Mission Point Resort on Mackinac Island and confirm our honeymoon? In two days, we'll be leaving the Chevy at the dock and ferrying away to an island with no cars and no worries. We'll rent bikes, take BW for long walks along the lake, drink beer and eat fried green beans--it's a thing up there. We'll pet the horses and buy fudge for all our friends. I bet they even have fudge with sprinkles and..." Boone looked down the hall toward the stairs. "Do you hear footsteps?"

"I think we're being burgled."

"I think we need to find a new hiding place for that key under the back mat." Boone came over and kissed the top of my head. "You deal with our intruder, and I'll deal with our honeymoon. We'll worry about moving when we get back. Hollis will have to wait."

Boone planted another kiss in my hair. "Are you sure there's nothing else going on? Not only are you one hot number, Sweet-hing, but you have the instincts of James Bond."

"Not Spiderman?"

"Spiderman doesn't drink martinis."

I made my way downstairs to Mamma coming through the kitchen, waving her credit card at me. "I was looking in on KiKi and noticed that arbor on your front porch. I want to buy it for Everett, it's just what he needs for his prize rose bush. It should fit in the Chevy if you put the top down and add some ropes to hold it in place."

"Really? This is it? I nearly get blown to smithereens, and you don't even ask how *I am*?"

"Like Cher says: 'All's well that ends well,' dear, and of course you're okay. You're standing right here in front of me, and if I asked how you were every time you got into a little scrape, we'd never have a decent conversation."

"I think that's Shakespeare."

"Cher, Shakespeare, it's all the same."

This from a woman on the board of directors for the Chatham County Library System?

"I mean, what do you give the man who has everything?" Mamma added with that dreamy look in her eyes again. "He is amazing in so many ways. I'll watch the shop, and you need to get a move on this morning while Everett's at the courthouse or it won't be a surprise. He does love surprises. He certainly knows how to surprise me. In fact, he told me this morning that he didn't think those two arrested for Corny's murder are guilty."

That got my attention. "Did he say why?"

Mamma blushed from head to chin. "I don't remember, dear. I was too busy being surprised by something else."

I didn't need to hear another word about surprises, so I wrote up the sale and headed for the garage to get the Chevy. Not wanting to drag Boone away from honeymoon plans, I pulled the Chevy to the front of Cherry House. I spread out an old comforter so as not to hurt the car, then Mamma and I manhandled, or in this case woman-handled, the arbor into the back seat. I tied it down. If I added greenery, I'd look like a float in the St. Patrick's parade.

Sleepy Pines was on the way to the judge's house, and Enos must be feeling bad about the arrest of his nephew and Emmi-lene. Corny was a bad guy and needed to be stopped, and Emmilene had every right to dislike her brother. Davis genuinely seemed to care about his uncle and hated what Corny did to him. It all added up. It all made perfect sense with the right motives and opportunity. Everything was tied up in a neat little package.

So why did Swain think Davis and Emmilene weren't guilty of doing in Corny? And why did a little piece of me, way deep down inside, agree with him?

CHAPTER 13

"Does your husband know you went and turned his swanky convertible into a U-Haul?" Enos pulled Rocket to a stop on the other side of the fence in front of Sleepy Pines, and I got out of the Chevy.

"It's a delivery for Mamma, and I thought I'd stop by and see how you're getting along." I held up a Cakery Bakery doughnut bag and carton holding two coffees. "Nice morning for a drive?"

"Nice morning for repair work. I'm one of the few people around here who knows one end of a hammer from the other. Besides, it's best I keep busy. The others are packing up for the Vegas trip, but I just can't get into it."

Cradling the wood pineapple finial that I'd knocked off a few days ago, Enos climbed from the cart. "Care to lend a hand?"

I propped the bag by the fence, set the coffees to the side and squared the freshly painted finial on top of the end post. Enos retrieved his toolbox from the cart and flipped it open. "Usually, Davis helps me with repairs around the place. But now, well, things are different now." Enos drilled a few holes, the whirl of the motor and bit cutting into the wood mixing with the noise of the light traffic up and down Tattnall. He added screws to secure the pineapple.

"There." Enos stood back and admired his handiwork. "Good as new. And the rest of the fence will follow in a few weeks."

I rounded the post to the other side and held out the doughnut bag. Enos snagged a coffee and a powdered sugar. I took a glazed. If I kept up my present doughnut habit, I'd weigh as much as Enos's golf cart by Christmas.

Enos and I sat in Rocket, enjoying the moment, leaves drifting down around us. "Sorry about all this." I took a bite. "About the fence, about Davis. I think he did what he did because Corny pushed him too far with the bribe and taking over IDD."

Enos gulped the coffee. "And Emmilene wanted her money. Hard for me to believe they'd kill Corny over an inheritance and some paintings. Then again, blackmail is an ugly game." Enos took another bite. "And as for the fence, Missy, you're not the first to take a swipe at it."

Enos added a little wink. "Back when this here house was built in 1888, all the pickets had little carved pineapples on the top. We found the pictures in the attic. Little by little, the fence rotted or got knocked over and was replaced by any old thing. When Jeb got hit back in April, we voted to put the whole shebang back the way it was in the first place. Give the place some class. We had the fence special made, too. Took seven months and cost a pretty penny. I'll have my work cut out getting it all put up," Enos added.

At least I think that's what he added because I wasn't listening. "April?"

"Yep. Something wrong with the doughnut? You stopped eating."

I turned in my seat and faced Enos. "What exactly happened with Jeb?"

"Terrible it was, just terrible. Around nine or so Jeb was walking home from that folk music concert at First Presbyterian. Best we can tell, a car jumped the curb and caught Jeb from behind. Poor old soul never knew what hit him. A bunch of us were on the back patio, having pies and pints--that's beer and apple pie. Anyway, we heard the commotion, and by the time we got to Jeb, Davis had already called 911 and was making Jeb comfortable. We were all in such a fluster that it was a mighty good thing my boy decided to stop by like he did."

"Was Corny there?"

"The rotten weasel...guess I shouldn't be speaking ill of the dead, but truth is truth. He was here loading up an oak end table to sell for Belinda Hayes. Said he didn't see a thing, but I don't know how he missed it. He was standing right there, playing with his fancy phone. Just like Corny, if it's not making him a fast buck, he doesn't care diddly about anyone else. The police didn't have a clue who hit Jeb. The fence was decrepit enough that one mark was like another."

I took a deep breath. "And Davis had his Jeep at that time?"

"He's had that thing forever. Big enough to do deliveries and got more dings than an alarm clock." Enos added a little chuckle then sobered. "Do you think Walker would be willing to take on Davis's and Emmilene's case? They're going to be needing a good lawyer with the mess they got themselves into."

"I'll ask Boone to give you a call. I need to get this arbor delivered, or Mamma will have my head." I stuffed the empty cups into the bag then climbed in the convertible. I forced a smile, gave a little wave and pulled away from the curb, feeling sick. It had nothing to do with doughnuts.

Corny wasn't just blackmailing Davis over the forgeries. He

was blackmailing Davis over the hit-and-run of Jeb Wilcox. The date fit, Davis was at the scene before anyone else, and he had the Jeep. And whereas...good grief, I was starting to think like a lawyer...Davis and Emmilene might not kill over the paintings and an inheritance, Corny was no doubt bleeding them dry with the threat of turning Davis into the police for the hit and run.

Davis took the Jeep picture from me at IDD, so now there was no evidence to tie him to the accident. Davis getting a lighter sentence because Corny was blackmailing him might help, but with a charge of hit-and-run added on, Davis would never see the light of day. So now what? Did I tell Boone? Did I *not* tell Boone? Jeb Wilcox deserved justice, but there was no evidence. I needed to talk to Mercedes. All that time spent with dead people gave her a unique way of looking at things.

With my head pounding and my hands sweating, I pulled into the driveway of the judge's lovely house, where all was peaceful and uncomplicated. I undid the rope holding the arbor and heaved it out of the car. Leaving it in plain sight would ruin Mamma's big surprise. I shoved Old Yeller onto my shoulder and hoisted the arbor back to the detached garage painted the same as the house. I didn't have the code for the garage opener, so I lugged the arbor--that was beginning to feel like a third leg-- to the side door. I found a key under the mat. Boone and I weren't the only ones needing to find a new hiding place for a spare key.

Elbowing open the door, I shoved the arbor through and flipped the light switch. It had a garage smell of fertilizer mixed with gas and oil and sawdust. A stack of boards sat to the left, workbench and table saw at the back, black Caddy on one side of the double car garage, and a black Jeep with a crumpled left fender right in front of me. I blinked a few times, half expecting it to evaporate. The Jeep was smaller with the canvas top. Taking it down made a convertible and easy to see the decal on the windshield. A yellow decal. A photo of a Jeep lay on the dashboard. It was the one snapped out of my hand at IDD.

I leaned in through the window to get the photo, and footsteps sounded at the door. I spun around to see Swain framed in the entrance. He stepped inside, his eyes widening. Without saying a word, he picked up a piece of two-by-four. My heart stopped dead in my chest. I flattened myself against the Jeep.

"Don't move," Swain whispered, slowly creeping closer, a determined set to his chin. "This will be over in a minute." He raised the board above his head. I closed my eyes and screamed bloody murder with the sound of the board smacking down again and again.

I pried one eye open. No choir of angels or pearly gates. Then again, there was no band of devils or pitchforks. I wasn't dead, but something long, thin, and dripping blood dangled from Swain's fingers.

"Copperhead. They're everywhere this time of year, looking for a place to winter, like the canvas top of a car. You interrupted his sleep, and he was sliding down to lunch on your pretty little neck."

Swain walked to the door and flung the remains out into the yard. When he turned back, I lunged at him, catching him midsection in a full body slam and smashing him against the garage wall with a solid *umph*.

"You rat!" Half crying, half screaming and totally pumped on adrenaline, I pounded Swain with both fists. "You no-good, stinking rat! This will break Mamma's heart! She loves you!"

Swain didn't even try to stop me. "She served her purpose."

I stepped back and swiped my nose with the back of my hand. "Wh...What's that mean?"

Swain folded his arms and nodded at the Jeep. "Yeah, I hit

Wilcox, and Corny got rich by not letting me forget it. You saw those overdue bills in my car. I was getting creamed. I took up with Gloria to cement my image as an upstanding man, courting an upstanding woman. It made framing KiKi for Corny's murder easy."

"And no one suspected the upstanding man dating her sister, who even drove to the airport, hunting down a suspect."

"Nice touch, if I do say so myself."

"You torched the auction house to get rid of the Jeep pictures."

"And then you show up. I was ditching the Jeep today, running it into the river, and you show up *again*. Aren't you supposed to be on a honeymoon?"

I looked back at the Jeep. "Mario Kart for real."

"They don't call me the Silver Fox for nothing, and as for Gloria, I can do a lot better than a prissy old widow. But like I said, she served her purpose."

Little red dots danced in front of my eyes. "Rot in hell, Swain." I pulled in a deep breath. "Now what? You beat me over the head like you did Corny and the snake?"

"You've been driving all over town with an arbor sticking out of a red '57 Chevy convertible, and it's parked right outside my house." Swain pulled out his phone and tossed it to me. "This was a big gamble the night I hit Wilcox and drove away. I'd been drinking, and it would have ended my career. I thought I could make this work. I even considered framing my no-good, loser stepson who never does anything right and has screwed up his life. Even that didn't work. Now you're here, and I've run out the clock. Time to call the cops."

"And what do I tell Mamma? She really does love you."

"Tell her it's like Cher says: 'Snap out of it.'"

.   .   .

"SNAP OUT OF IT? SNAP OUT OF IT!" MAMMA THREW AN ANTIQUE vase that I'd just taken in for consignment across the room. The yellow bone china smashed into a bazillion pieces against the wall by the hat display. BW dove under the dining room display table, and Auntie KiKi continued to sip tea without spilling a drop.

"I'm going down to that police station, and I'll show Judge Everett Swain what 'snap' really is. I'll snap his mangy neck, wear red at his funeral, and dance on his grave!"

"Mamma, I know you're hurt, but you're better than that."

"You are so right! First, I'll set his silver hair on fire, punch his brown lights out, kick his arthritic knee, *then* snap his mangy neck."

Mamma stormed toward the door and grabbed her purse off the checkout counter with me barely acing her out at the entrance. I spread my arms and legs, forming a human shield across the threshold. "If you go to the station, Scarlett Rose and every media outlet from here to Atlanta will have you as their lead story for a month."

"I don't give a flying fig about the media. That man is not going to lead me on for seven months, toss me to the curb like some old rag and think he can get away with it. No woman worth her pearls would hold still for such treatment, especially not Judge Gloria Summerside."

"I've been thinking," Auntie KiKi said while holding her teacup with pinky extended, "Swain is more a BMW man or a Mercedes man or maybe even into one of those new Tesla cars coming out, but a Jeep?"

"The man has a wild side, okay?" Mamma fumed. "A very wild side that I have no intention of going into at the moment. But if I get my way, his wild is coming to an end right quick, and he'll be talking with a high, squeaky voice for the rest of his natural life."

Auntie KiKi dabbed her lips with a lace napkin that was now no longer suitable for consignment. She sallied up next to Mamma, linked her arm and drew close. "Just making sure that's the way you really feel, sister dear. If you want Judge Swain, we'll get him. Summerside girls stick together, and I do feel the need for a bit of good ol' reality TV. Something about Corny and his double-dealing ways and the people he's hurt should do the trick. If I throw in Great-Granddaddy's shotgun and two holes in my ceiling--everybody loves a good shotgun story--I'll go viral."

Auntie KiKi gave Mamma a kiss on the cheek. "That should be distraction enough for the media and let you sneak in the back door of station without a fuss. You know the police there, and they'll surely grant you a few private minutes, considering the circumstances. Besides, Putter doesn't get home till midnight, and what am I supposed to do with myself till then?"

I looked from Mamma to Auntie KiKi. "I'm coming with."

Mamma shook her head. "We need a getaway car."

"Oh, good grief."

She tossed me the keys to the Caddy. "Go to Everett-the-jack-ass's house and get my things. The garage might be cordoned off with police tape, but the house should be okay. The only crime committed there was me believing that smooth-talking, lily-livered, sanctimonious butthead. Pick KiKi and me up at the station in an hour. The security alarm code is my birthday. My evening dress is in the upstairs closet with my fall coat and some other clothes. Get my hairdryer and my new electric toothbrush with rotating bristles for healthier gums. I want my toothbrush."

I looked from Mamma to Auntie KiKi. "This is crazy."

"When you get back to the station, flip the headlights twice, so we know it's you."

"You got a black Cadillac with a *U DID IT* license plate. You'll know."

"If anything goes amiss, Walker's already there, trying to

make sense of this mess. With a little luck, he's flattened Butthead at least twice for me."

I got in the driver's seat of the Caddy, and Mamma took passenger. Auntie KiKi and BW slipped into the backseat. I dropped the troublemakers off on President Street. Their plan was to cut through Telfair Square, take the alley behind Flying Monkey Noodle Bar, and across to the back of the police station without being ambushed by the press. That the three of us knew the ins and outs of the station so well suggested the Summerside girls were a feisty lot and then some.

BW claimed his seat beside me and stuck his head out the window. Two minutes later, we parked across the street from Swain's driveway so as not to draw attention from busybody neighbors. We went around to the back door, did the key and code thing to disengage the alarm and went inside. Not turning on the lights, I pulled out my flashlight. I cut through the kitchen and trotted up the stairway with BW right behind me.

First bedroom on the right had to be the master with a crystal chandelier, custom drapes, and nightstand with Mamma's picture. BW charged past me landing paws-out right in the middle of the king-size, four-poster bed.

"Don't get any highfalutin ideas, pup-o. This is filet mignon territory, and we are hamburger and mac and cheese. But Mamma would have been happy here." I looked around. "She *was* happy here."

BW stretched out as if he belonged, and I plopped my purse beside him. I found an overnight bag in the walk-in closet sporting one of those fancy organizer units. I folded in Mamma's clothes, wrapped her shoes in one of Swain's denim shirts and added them to the case. I headed for the master bathroom right out of HGTV when a crash came from the first floor.

Burglars? BW didn't budge. It would have taken more than burglars and a stick of dynamite to get him off a silk down comforter. I'd heard about thieves keeping track of arrests. They figured the house was empty and ripe for the pickings, especially a house belonging to a well-to-do judge. Swain's bedroom was low on weaponry unless you considered Mamma's toothbrush. I grabbed an umbrella from the closet and tippy-toed down the stairs toward the light coming from the living room.

CHAPTER 14

"Simon?"

He spun around, sending papers flying off the desk. "You're the woman from that Fox place. What the heck are you doing here?"

"Well," I said as I walked into the room, picking up the papers as I went. "Everett and my mother are...were an item, and I came to get her things and--"

Simon waved his hand, cutting me off. He turned back to the antique desk with a large writing area and carved drawers. "I don't care what your mother's up to with Loser Boy, but since you're here, make yourself useful. Take all his clothes from upstairs and sell them."

"Uh, he hasn't even gone to trial yet." I put the papers on the table under the family photo wall of Christmases, first bike, Halloween, graduation, vacations, quarterback and the like.

"Take the furniture too," Simon said while slamming one drawer after the other. "Except for the antiques, I'll get a buyer for them, then I'm selling this mausoleum. Where the heck's the money? Loser Boy always keeps cash in one of these drawers."

"Have you been to see your dad?"

"My dad died when I was ten. He was loaded, not some flunky judge. Next month, I won't be scrounging in drawers. Next month, I turn thirty."

"A milestone birthday." I sat on the arm of one of the side chairs. "When I turned thirty, I inherited money. A trust fund from my grandmother. I had to graduate from college to get it. If I got into trouble, the trust was revocable. You quarterbacked for the Gators?"

Simon pulled out another drawer. "Now that's what I'm talking about." He wadded bills into a roll and stuffed them in his front jeans pocket. "Okay, time to go, Ms. Foxy. Come back tomorrow and get the rest."

I didn't budge. "So, how was it? Did you go crying to Everett, knowing he'd pay your overdue bills and bail you out? The loans, the overdrawn accounts. Corny had you over a barrel, and he was taking you for all you were worth."

Simon slowly turned, his eyes cold, jaw set.

"You were borrowing against your inheritance," I went on, "to pay Corny off. Soon there'd be nothing left. You hit Jeb Wilcox. Corny saw it. You killed Cornelius McBride."

I yanked the quarterback photo from the wall and threw it at Simon. "Your black hoodie with an alligator. The Florida Gators. You torched the auction house to get rid of the pictures. Everett has a bad knee. He couldn't have gotten up on the back roof. KiKi found Snickers on the living room floor. It dropped out of your pocket when you were at her house. Candy from Jen's and Friends."

"Everett confessed. Case closed."

"Everett took the fall because you're his family. He felt like he failed you, and there is nothing more important to Judge Everett Swain than family."

"You know what else the good old judge keeps in this desk." Simon reached into a drawer and pulled out a gun. "It's not big, but it'll do the trick against an intruder. You're the intruder."

Out of the corner of my eye, I caught a reflection in the mirror. Boone was outside the window.

"Everett had it all figured out," Simon continued while Boone gave me hand signals that I didn't understand. We needed to learn sign language.

"I told him how I needed him, how he was such a great dad, and all that other crap. Loser Boy said he'd fix it. I thought he'd ditch the Jeep somewhere, but a confession is a whole lot neater. Ties up all those pesky loose ends. You, Ms. Foxy, are a loose end."

BW wandered into the living room and gave a big doggie stretch. Wagged his tail, he came toward Simon, looking for a pet.

"Not much of a guard dog."

"BW: the canine version of the Dalai Lama." I clapped my hands to get BW's attention, hoping he'd come to me and not see Boone. "Come here, boy."

I clapped again just as BW tore straight for the window, barking and wagging his tail so hard I thought it might fly off.

Simon turned to the window, and I lunged for him. He grabbed me by the neck and aimed the gun at my head. "Whoever you are out there, if you want to keep Foxy and this dog alive, you better get in here fast."

I heard the back door open and footsteps I knew as well as my own in the hall. My heart thudded in time with the steps, my brain racing, trying to figure out what to do. Boone came into view, BW beside him, just as the front door banged open with Auntie Kiki bellowing, "Reagan!" and Mamma chiming in with "It's been over and hour, and my feet are killing me, and you were supposed to--"

Simon jerked the gun toward the front door.

I elbowed him hard in the ribs; Boone grabbed the gun, adding a gut punch; and BW licked Simon's face as he thrashed about on the floor like a landed fish.

"What in the world is going on?" Mamma gasped as Auntie KiKi took the gun from Boone.

"Simon's guilty. Everett's innocent." I helped Boone cinch Simon's hands together behind his back, using Boone's belt that I'd given him for his birthday.

"Well, then it's a mighty good thing I told Walker you were here," Mamma said. "And I know about the innocent part." She sat on the couch, kicked off her shoes and rubbed her foot. "I saw the police report. The Jeep's a stick shift. Everett has trouble finding Park in an automatic. And you," Mamma threw a shoe at Simon, bouncing it off his head, "should be ashamed of yourself."

Auntie KiKi stuck the gun in her waistband and headed for the kitchen. I sat on Simon's butt to keep him in place. One advantage of all those doughnuts.

"How did *you* know Everett didn't do it?" I asked Boone.

"You were still alive." Boone gave me a kiss and ripped a cord from a really expensive table lamp. "If Everett was the killer, he would have killed you and tried to get away. That's what the bad guys do. They don't hang around and call the cops." Boone tied Simon's legs. "I talked to Everett. He told me about the snake. He's not one of the bad guys."

"Did you hear that, Mamma?" I called over my shoulder. "Not a bad guy."

"I'm still getting over 'snap out of it.'"

Sirens sounded in the distance, and Auntie KiKi came in with a silver tray and chilled pitcher plus martini glasses and skewered olives. "The man of the house keeps a mighty fine liquor cabinet I'll give him that. With a little luck and some good vodka, I think we can salvage this here night after all."

. . .

BY NINE THE NEXT MORNING, BOONE HAD THE CHEVY LOADED with luggage and doggie paraphernalia. I checked the hose one more time to make sure I'd completely turned it off and not have it dripping for two weeks when I spied Hollis headed up the walk, balancing boxes. "We were so close," Boone said to me.

"Hollis is my problem. I'm the one who married him."

I met Hollis on the walk and snagged the top box. "You can't move in for two weeks, remember. Come hell or high water, I'm going on my honeymoon."

"Yeah, yeah, yeah, I hear you," Hollis said. "But you won't be around to stop me." He kicked open the front door. "Lou Ella's decided to tear off this front porch and add something modern. For sure we're cutting down that stupid cherry tree. How old is that thing anyway?"

Protest was useless. Cherry House wasn't my house. I followed Hollis through the entrance hall with my new checkout counter, past the dining room with displays and racks I'd built myself, then into the kitchen with the little dressing rooms converted from the pantry. I put my box by the others. Hollis did the same, knocking one over and scattering the contents across the floor.

"Just look at all those family heirlooms." Hollis spread his arms wide. "So much to be proud of." He stooped down and laid out the military medals and dog tags nice and neat. "Here's Mother's birth certificate." He put it beside the tags. "Here's the chart from *23andMe* showing everything about Mamma and the old established families of Savannah we're related to." Hollis put it next to the birth certificate.

"Hollis, this is your blood donor card." I held it up. "You gave once, passed out cold and thought you were going to die."

Hollis grabbed the card, smoothed it out and put it next to

the chart. "They took a lot of blood that day. B positive is very rare. The nurse told me so, and that card's going on the hall wall, showing I do my part. I'm having the wall framed in and--"

"Oh, boy."

"Framing will look good, especially when the crest is done."

"Look closer. You daddy's blood type is O negative." I held up the tags. "The chart says," I picked it up in my other hand, "that your mamma's O negative. You're B positive. Blood types are not algebra, Hollis. Two negatives do not make a positive."

Hollis sat back on his heels then plopped flat on the floor. His jaw dropped, and his eyes glazed. Hollis didn't move for a full minute. "No. My mamma? My daddy isn't...isn't... I'm not a..."

"You don't have to display all this. Just use the flag and the crest, that makes a good design."

"But you know."

I held out the tags and the chart. "I'll trade you these and a bad memory for one Cakery Bakery receipt."

"But...But Lou Ella really likes this house."

"Lou Ella likes being a Beaumont more. And you still have the glory of not throwing the Vanderpools out of their house. Think of the Telfair Christmas ball, the invitation to the yacht club."

"How could you do this to me?"

"Hey, I did you a favor. If you had displayed the tags and the chart and the doner card..."

"What do I tell Lou Ella?"

"Tell her Cherry House is haunted. Tell her it's built over a sinkhole. Tell her a Yankee general slept here."

"That'll do it." Hollis fished his wallet from his back pocket and gingerly unfolded the receipt. He handed it over, and I put the chart and tags back in the box.

"I'll get these things later." Hollis stood and gazed around. "I was so close to getting this house. I really wanted it."

"Yeah, me too."

Hollis plodded his way through the house and out the front door. I followed and did a two-step over to Boone, leaning against the car, and BW sitting beside him. I did a swirl and added a pirouette left over from ballet classes. I held up the Cakery Bakery receipt and waved it in the air. "Home sweet home is still our home sweet home."

I tore up the paper, gave it a toss, and let the slivers rain down over the three of us like confetti.

"How?"

"Bad blood." I threw my arms around Boone and kissed him hard. "Mackinac Island, here we come. Three days up, three days back, eight days on a real island with no cars and only bikes and horses and fudge and fried green beans. So much to look forward to, husband dear. What could possibly go wrong for newlyweds in paradise?

BAKING WITH AUNTIE KIKI

Baking with Auntie KiKi
(with or without martini in hand)

Auntie KiKi's baking tips that really work.

-Use metal pans for baking. Metal transfers heat much better than glass and makes the batter lighter.

-Always sift flour. Makes for lighter and tastier pastries. If you don't have a sifter run the flour through a colander. This works just as well.

-Ingredients at room temperature. If you forget to take out the eggs and milk, run under warm water till they no longer feel cold.

-Parchment paper when baking cookies or when you want to be sure a cake comes out of the pan.

AUNTIE KIKI'S TO-DIE-FOR BLUEBERRY MUFFINS

Ingredients
- 1 ½ cup flour
- ¾ cup brown sugar
- ½ teaspoon salt
- 2 teaspoons baking powder
- 1 teaspoon vanilla
- 1 teaspoon cinnamon
- ¼ teaspoon nutmeg
- 1/3 cup vegetable oil
- 1 egg
- 1/3 cup buttermilk
- 1 cup blueberries (fresh or frozen)

Topping:
- ½ cup brown sugar
- 1/3 cup flour
- 3 or 4 Tablespoons cubed butter (not softened)
- 1 ½ teaspoon cinnamon

*Use the adorable high collar muffin papers for best results

Preheat oven to 400

Combine 1½ cup flour, ¾ cup brown sugar, salt, baking powder. Mix.

Place vegetable oil in a 1-cup measuring cup, add the egg slightly beaten, fill the rest of the way with the buttermilk to make one full cup. Combine with a fork then mix all this into the flour mixture. Use a big spoon and do not overmix. Fold in blueberries.

Crumb topping:

Mix ½ cup brown sugar, 1/3 cup flour, 1½ teaspoon cinnamon. Add the cubed butter and mush together with your fingers to make crumbles.

Fill muffin cups to top of where the muffin tin stops. (about an inch and a half high) Put crumbles on top.

Bake 25 minutes.

AUNTIE KIKI'S AWARD-WINNING RAZZLEBERRY PIE

Yes, it really is that good!

3 c blackberries
   2 c raspberries
   1 ½ blueberries
   1 c sugar
   ½ t salt
   ¼ c instant tapioca
   2 tablespoons lemon juice
   *Use nonstick pan sprayed as these pies get sticky

Gently mix all above and dump into pie crust
   Lattice the top crust, brush with egg whites, sprinkle with coarse sugar.
   Bake 425 for 15 min with edges covered with aluminum foil to keep from burning.
   Drop to 350, take off foil, bake for 30-35 min (till top is brown)
   Let sit for a few hours to set up.
   **How to make a lattice-top pie crust. Make your own crust or, like Auntie KiKi does when in a hurry, buy Pillsbury crusts.

Roll out one crust and use for bottom

Roll out second crust on a floured surface, cut into one-inch strips using a pizza cutter. Works really well.

-Lay strips one inch apart across top of pie

-Fold back every other strip

-Lay in a crust strip going the other direction.

-Fold down the original strips

-Fold back the alternating strips

-Lay in another strip then fold down the strips folded up.

And so on across the top of the pie

BOOKS BY DUFFY BROWN

Consignment Shop Mysteries

Iced Chiffon

Killer in Crinolines

Pearls and Poison

Dead Man Walker

Demise in Denim

Lethal in Old Lace

Wedding Day and Foul Play

Cycle Path Mysteries

Braking for Bodies

Tandem Demise

Made in the USA
Middletown, DE
08 May 2024

54050648R00096